The Space Between Our Tears

JOHN REGAN

ISBN-10: 978-1728659039

DEDICATION

For Mam. For everything.

ACKNOWLEDGMENTS

It goes without saying that to produce anything worthwhile, requires help from others. The process of writing a book such as this is aided and abetted by numerous people. Some of who only subtly assist, and others, who profoundly do so. My thanks go to anyone who however small, has contributed to this novel. My main appreciation, however, is to the people who purchased and read my first three books: The Hanging Tree, Persistence of Vision and The Romanov Relic. Your support is greatly appreciated. Many thanks go to my writing friends – The Monday Horsemen – for their invaluable support and help in making this book possible. Finally, to anyone who is reading this book. I hope you find it enjoyable, and any feedback is always appreciated.

September 2017.

DISCLAIMER

Many of the places mentioned in this book exist. However, the author has used poetic license throughout, to maintain an engaging narrative. Therefore, no guarantee of accuracy in some respects should be expected. The characters depicted, however, are wholly fictional. Any similarity to persons living or dead is accidental.

THE SPACE BETWEEN OUR TEARS

If tears are the manifestation of our grief. What lies within the space between them?

The gathering storm appears, across our line of sight.
A thundering irresistible force, of magnitude and might.
Pushing easily past defences, we erected for the fight.
And happiness a stranger, as all our hopes take flight.

As darkness pushes daylight, and blackness grips once more.
Its power and strength colossus, impossible to ignore.
Shattering everything before it, on the journey to our core.
Depositing crumpled memories, upon a deserted shore

A desolate land of sorrow, with words that no one hears
Where loneliness finds comfort and recollection sears
A place where none would wish to live, the home to darkest fears
Battered, bruised and broken, in the space between our tears.

JOURNAL OF EMILY G KIRKBY

*I decided some time ago to put down my thoughts and commit them to a diary. It's a decision made one day while trying to begin the writing of my first novel – **Their Journals.** Having set out on this journey, what started off as a relatively easy thing to do, changed my whole outlook on life.*

If you are embarking on something like this, I believe in total honesty. This may seem at first a natural choice to make, but it's only when you see your thoughts laid bare, you fully understand the enormity of them. When looking back at what I've written, it surprises me I was able to do this. Some days are of course, more prosaic. While others, even now, are heartbreaking to read back.

We don't live our lives in isolation. Continuously coming into contact with many people. The tectonic plates of life. Often when these plates collide with others, mountains are raised and tsunamis launched.

Some of what I've done in life I'm deeply ashamed of. Some I've greatly regretted. But having decided long-ago, however, that what's done is done. An acceptance that the past cannot be altered and when the wheels are set in motion, we must suffer our fate. Regret is a foolish enterprise, of course. A belief, given our time again, we would live our life differently. We wouldn't. The people we are, the person I am, is a result of the choices made back then, not in spite of them. We are in effect, the sum total of the experiences we have had.

It doesn't mean I'm indifferent to these events or indeed the people I've encountered, the individuals who have shaped and moulded Emily G. Kirkby into the person she is today. I need to reach a resolution within myself, though. I have the rest of my life to lead, and if I'm going to be of any use to the people who love me, it's something I must continually strive to do.

My story is a rich and vibrant one. Full of the things in life that genuinely matter. It's a story about love, in all its varied guises. A story about loss and bereavement, about regret and remorse, guilt and redemption. But mainly, chiefly, it's about love. Without which any of us are incapable of functioning. To love, to be loved, are truly, the greatest gifts life can bestow on us.

EMILY G. KIRKBY - 2017

CHAPTER ONE

EMILY - NOVEMBER 2013 - Another day, another train journey. I don't know when I began to despise them. Those lost two and a half hours spent travelling to London. What once seemed a necessity and an opportunity to catch up on work, had now become a chore. The early morning rise, usually on the back of a bottle of wine consumed the night before. The scrambling around for clothing, toiletries, hairdryer and makeup. The hastily packed suitcase stuffed with clothing and shoes I wouldn't wear once there. The fear as I raced from the house – jumping into the taxi – that I'd forgotten something vital. The mundane conversation with the driver about where I was heading, and what I would be doing when I got there. Paul resented it too. The early days of our relationship, when he'd get up with me and cook breakfast, long gone. Now he would roll over and go back to sleep if I happened to wake him from his slumber. I worried what he did while I was away. Our two lives only partially overlapping in a bizarre-relationship Venn diagram. Maybe he worried about me too. I doubted it. Not even attempting to disguise his marked detachment. Returning to Teesside was at one time exciting, the days spent apart creating a frisson of passion between us, now dissolved into a polar indifference. We had drifted apart and fell out of love. Cliché piled on cliché described our relationship nowadays. He was distant, light-years away. Our sex life, perfunctory. Where words filled the air around us, silence now reigned. The telephone calls to him while away, dwindling from an hour-long chat to minutes, and finally decaying into texts, until these too, atrophied and died. I longed and ached for something new and thrilling. To feel the long-lost stranger of excitement shake me from my emotional inertia. Would Paul and I return to the halcyon days of our past? I didn't know. The slowly receding embers of our love all but extinguished. The thing which could have brought us closer, gone, expunged from my life.

I watched as bodies boarded and alighted from the train. The noise, the suffocating closeness of people I didn't know and never would. The stations and scenery flashed by in a mixture of boredom and annoyance. A whiny voice, a constant cough, the low drum of deafening music partially muted by headphones. Disgusting coffee and poor-quality, overpriced food. The pushing and jostling as we reached King's Cross. I slumped onto the seat as the taxi driver placed my luggage in the boot. Feigning looking at my mobile to avoid another dose of inane chatter. As the vehicle stopped outside my place of work, I got out and stared up at the building. A thought chugged into my mind. A seed which germinated and grew until the idea, a realisation, washed over me. Today would be a day of change. Today would be a new beginning. Bursting through the doors of the publishing house with renewed hope. London, trains, shit coffee, teeth-gritting inducing commuters, tedious taxi drivers and everything between Darlington and King's Cross, would be no more.

My journey back home was much better. Like a ponderous weight eased from my shoulders. Feeling upbeat, excited and apprehensive. A legion of butterflies swirled inside of me as I mentally extrapolated my future. Scenario after scenario flooded my mind in a tremendous imaginary deluge. Some of them optimistic, others not. The doubts which elbowed their way into my head now pushed aside. I wouldn't weaken. I couldn't. To change my mind would seem like defeat. What would I do from this point onward? I didn't know. Return home and tell Paul I suppose. How would he react when his bit-part lover turned full-time? Would it be the end of us or a new beginning? A part of me loved him. Wanting the cold coals of our relationship to spring back to life. The breath of our passion blowing on the embers, re-igniting the flame.

A taxi ride followed the train and finally pulled up outside my flat. A blank space where Paul generally parked his car greeted me. I sighed with relief. The inevitable conversation I would need to have with him, shunted into a siding for the time being. Dropping my suitcase, I threw my coat over the bannister, and leaning back against the door, drew in a breath. As my heart-rate approached something resembling ordinary, I smiled and closed my eyes. Allowing myself a moment to reflect on what I had done. The doubts I had about my new life, although still there, seemed to have softened. I wandered into the living room and through to the kitchen. A glass of wine to toast a new beginning. Then, with a drink in hand, I caught sight of the note resting against the vase on the table.

Dear Emily, it began ...

ONE WEEK LATER - Emily followed the waiter as he slalomed his way across the restaurant. Arriving at a table, she sat. The waiter smiled, Emily forced a superficial one of her own. He handed her the menu, depositing a second in front of the seat opposite. Taking out his notepad, he waited.

Emily glanced up at him. 'Can I have a glass of—' Holding up a finger as the mobile in her handbag sounded.

She read the text from Lisa: *Running late. I'll be five minutes. Order me a drink. Xx.*

Replacing the phone, she fixed her attention back to the waiter. 'Sorry about that. My friend's a little late. Can I have two glasses of Pinot Grigio, please?'

'Of course.' He scribbled down her order. The waiter smiled again and left.

Emily waited in silence, glancing around the mostly empty room. A spartan number of customers scattered around on different tables. She picked up the menu and perused. Already knowing what she would order. The waiter returned with two glasses and placed them on the table, smiling, he turned and headed towards the door as a couple entered. Emily watched as a brief conversation took place before they followed the waiter to a table close to her own. The woman smiled at her, a warm, genuine smile. Emily forced her face into something approaching a smile, and continued to watch the couple as they ordered their drinks. Attempting to conceal the fact she was observing them, by raising her menu higher.

Her attention moved away from them only when she spotted her friend enter. She waved at Lisa who hurried across to join her. The pair of them kissed as Lisa positioned herself opposite Emily.

Lisa picked up her glass, raised her eyebrows at Emily, and took a large swig. 'I need this.'

Emily peered over her friend's shoulder at the couple. 'Hard day?'

'Yeah. Bloody kids. Why did I become a teacher? Anyway, enough of my moaning. How are you?'

'Fine,' Emily said.

'Mmm. If you're fine, why are we here? Wednesday is our day. Today's Monday.'

Emily smiled. 'Nothing's set in stone, Lisa.' She took a sip of wine.

'Fine. I'll tell you all about my shitty day then.'

'Feel free.' Returning her gaze to the couple.

'What are you staring at?'

Emily grabbed her friends arm and tugged on it. 'Don't make it obvious.'

'Make what?' She turned back around to face Emily again.

'I'm watching a couple, that's all,' Emily said. 'People watching.'

Lisa clasped hold of her friend's hands. '*Emily,* what's up?'

Emily leant back in her chair and studied her friend. 'Paul's gone.'

'Gone? Gone where?'

'He left. I came back from London on Friday, and he'd gone.'

'What happened?'

Emily sighed. 'I'm not sure.'

'But did you expect it? Did he say he was going?'

'No. I went away, and when I returned he was gone. Along with all his stuff.'

'Didn't he phone or text?'

'He left a dear Emily letter. Usual. It's not you, it's me shite.'

'When did you last talk with him?'

'Tuesday night. Before I left home.'

Lisa peered up at the approaching waiter. 'Are you ready to order?' he said. His pad and pen poised.

Lisa handed him the menu. 'Chicken and mushroom risotto please.'

Emily emptied her glass. 'I'll have the carbonara and another wine.'

'Of course.' The waiter accepted the menu from Emily, finished writing, nodded at the two women and left.

Lisa stared at Emily. 'And he didn't give any hint he was thinking of leaving?'

'Not really. He'd been distant of late, but I just thought it was work stuff. You know Paul, deep as the ocean.'

'Are you sure he's not coming back? It may not be—'

Emily scoffed. 'He hired a van. The woman next door broke her neck to tell me. He'd clearly been planning it for some time.'

'Is there someone else?'

'I don't know. He didn't mention anyone but he wouldn't, would he?'

'Have you phoned him?'

'What's the point? This time next week he'll be in the States.'

'The States?'

'He received a job offer,' Emily said. 'He mentioned it weeks ago but didn't seem keen. I assumed he'd decided to turn it down.'

'I see.' The waiter returned with Emily's wine. 'Thanks,' Lisa said.

Lisa nodded towards her friend's already half-empty glass, raising her eyebrows. 'Are you just going to get pissed?'

Emily held her drink aloft. 'I might. Sobriety isn't what it's cracked up to be.'

Lisa put a hand on Emily's. 'Emily. Getting drunk is never the answer. I don't want to lecture—'

'You're a teacher, you always lecture. It's in your nature. Didactic. That's you.'

Lisa took her hand away and picked up her glass allowing herself a long sip. 'I'm sorry, I—'

'I had an abortion,' interrupted Emily. Her comment rolled across the table like a verbal hand grenade.

Lisa put down her glass and edged closer to her friend. 'You were pregnant. Why didn't you tell me?'

'It wasn't many weeks. I know how you feel about abortions. I ...' Emily momentarily closed her eyes and blew out her cheeks.

Lisa took hold of her friend's hand again. 'I'm not bothered about that. I have my views on abortions, but it's up to the woman. Your choice. I'd never pressurise you to do something you didn't want. I'm your best friend. I would understand.'

'I felt,' Emily struggled to find the words. 'Embarrassed.'

'Did Paul know?' Lisa said.

'Of course. He ...' She reached into her handbag for a tissue.

'He what?' Lisa said. Gently squeezing Emily's free hand.

'He convinced me it was for the best. He persuaded me it wasn't the right time to start a family and ...'

'The bastard,' Lisa hissed. 'He gets you to have an abortion and then pisses off.'

'It was my choice, Lisa. I didn't have to do it. I decided. Anyway, it's done. Fete Accompli.' Emily screwed up the tissue and threw it on the table turning her head away from her friend.

'And now?'

She faced Lisa again. 'And now I wish I hadn't.' She picked her glass back up as the waiter approached.

'Risotto?' Putting it in front of Lisa. She smiled at the waiter. 'Thanks.'

'And a carbonara.' Placing the plate down. 'Can I get you some parmesan or black pepper?'

'I'm all right,' Lisa said.

'Me too,' Emily said. 'I'll have another wine though.'

Lisa tutted at her friend as the waiter thanked the pair, and left them to it.

The two women ate their food, a silence descending across the table. Emily pushed small forkfuls into her mouth occasionally stopping to take a sizeable sip of wine.

Lisa paused. 'I'm supposed to be going out with Tim tonight. I can put him off if you like? He won't mind.'

Emily forced a smile. 'It's okay. I'll be fine.'

'I know but—'

'I'm not suicidal, Lisa.'

'I never said you were, but I do think you could use some company.'

'Go with Tim. You two hardly ever go out these days. I'll get through this. With the help of a few more of these.' Holding up her glass.

Lisa creased her brow. 'If you're sure.' She placed a hand on Emily's arm before quickly removing it.

'They're in love,' Emily said.

'Who?'

'The couple behind you.' Lisa turned. Emily grabbed hold of her arm. 'Don't look at them.'

'Why not? How can I tell if I don't? I don't even know what they look like.'

Emily smiled. 'I'll describe them.'

Lisa shook her head. 'They've probably just met. You know what it's like at the beginning of relationships. You can't take your eyes or keep your hands off each other. Someone told me years ago, once you've seen each other on the toilet the magic's gone.'

Emily screwed up her face. 'Lisa. I'm eating.'

'Describe them.' Lisa took a mouthful of food before pushing the half-full plate away from herself.

'She's about thirty,' Emily said. 'Maybe thirty-one or two. Pretty.'

'And the man?'

'Older. Early-forties I'd say.' Emily tilted her head a little. 'Handsome.'

Lisa drained her glass. 'Electra complex.'

Emily laughed. 'He's not old enough to be her dad.'

'As I said, they've probably just met.'

'Why can't I meet someone like that?'

'Emily,' Lisa said. Pulling her friend's attention back to her.

'I'm all right.' She gestured towards a passing waiter who stopped nearby. 'Can I have another two glasses of Pinot Grigio please?'

The waiter smiled. 'Of course.' And left.

Lisa blew out hard. 'This is my last. I don't want to arrive home pissed.'

Emily fixed Lisa with a stare. 'I've handed in my notice.'

Lisa threw herself back in her chair, her mouth dropping open. 'I don't believe you. I don't see you for a week and your whole life changes.'

'I'm sick of travelling all the time. Going up and down the east-coast-line a couple of days a week is soul destroying. So, I marched into Ruth's office and told her I was leaving.'

'What did the miserable bitch say?'

'Offered me more money.' She held out her hand and plucked the glass from the waiter as he arrived back at their table. Emily pushed the plate away from herself.

The waiter placed the second glass in front of Lisa. 'Can I get the dessert menu for you ladies?'

Emily smiled. 'I'll have the one with the most chocolate in it.'

The waiter laughed. 'Ok.' Making a note on his pad.

'I'm fine,' Lisa said.

The waiter focussed on Emily. 'Death by chocolate?' Raising his eyebrows for confirmation.

'That'll do. With cream. Lots of it.'

'Of course.' Collecting their plates, he left

'How much more?' Lisa asked.

'Five grand a year.'

'Jesus. I wish someone would offer me a wage rise like that.'

'I turned her down. It's done. I've got a bit of holiday left so, I only have another week there. Then I'm free.'

'Anything else you want to tell me? While you're unburdening yourself.'

'No. I think that's it.'

Lisa shook her head. 'How will you manage without working?'

'Paul said, in his letter, he's passed the flat over to me. He's written off his share. So, I don't have that to worry about.'

Lisa nodded slowly. 'That's the guilt he's feeling over …'

'Well, whatever it is. It's mine. I have some papers to sign. That's all.'

Lisa tapped her friend's hand. 'He must have been planning this for some time. I bet there's another woman.'

'Oh my God,' Emily said.

'What?'

'He's going to propose.'

'Not that couple again. Can I at least look?'

'You might as well. Everyone else is.'

Lisa spun around to see the man on one knee next to the woman. He held in his hand a ring which she accepted from him. The people and staff in the restaurant applauded as the woman blushed. The couple kissed, and the man returned to his seat.

Emily took a large swig of wine. 'Ruins your theory.'

Lisa frowned. 'What theory?'

'That they've just met. Nobody proposes on a first date.'

'I didn't say it was their first date.'

Emily lounged back in her chair and lifted the glass to her lips stopping short of her mouth. 'I'm going to write a book.'

'Really?' Lisa smiled. But realising Emily's seriousness, she shook her head. '*Really.*'

'I've always wanted to. You know that. I have excellent contacts. Publishers and such like.'

'You'll need a story,' Lisa said. 'It's sort of sine qua non.'

'I know, I know. I'm looking for ideas.'

'And until you write this best-seller?'

'I'll live off my savings.'

Lisa smiled and shook her head again. 'How long will they last?'

'A few years.' She took another large swig of wine.

'What genre?'

'I thought.' Emily burped. 'Excuse me. A love story.'

'Can't see you dressed in pink with a small dog on your lap.'

'Not that type of story. Mine will be a modern romance. Contemporary and up to date. I'm going to write a love story to end all love stories.' The last sentence sang.

Lisa drained her glass. 'You're drunk.'

Emily pointed at Lisa's empty glass. 'Another?' The waiter approached with her dessert and placed it in front of her.

Lisa put a hand on her glass. 'No more for me. I think you've had quite enough too.'

Emily produced a pet lip. 'Yes, Miss.'

'I'm only thinking of your liver.'

Emily picked up her spoon and smiled at Lisa. 'Would you like to try some?'

'No thanks. My blood pressure's rising just looking at it.'

Emily tucked in. Spoonful followed spoonful as she devoured the sweet. She placed the spoon on the empty plate, wiped her mouth with a napkin, and leant back in her seat.

'Happy?' Lisa asked.

'Blissfully. It's wonderful how chocolate lifts the mood.'

'That'll be the wine.'

The couple on the next table stood and made their way over to a desk near the door. Emily watched as the man shook hands with a waiter, paid their bill, and then the two of them left.

'I wonder how they met?' Emily said.

Lisa removed her mobile from her bag, studied it momentarily, and then put it back. 'Who?'

'The couple.'

'Who knows?'

'I bet their life's interesting. Maybe it would make a fantastic book.'

Lisa plucked her purse from her bag. 'You don't know anything about them. It's probably quite prosaic.'

Emily tapped her friend's hand. 'My treat. You can pay on Wednesday.'

Lisa raised her eyebrows. 'We're still doing Wednesday then? Twice in one week.'

'Absolutely. You can't mess with convention. It's the law,' Emily slurred. She stood. 'I'll go and pay for our meals.' And made her way across to the desk. Returning moments later she flopped down on her seat.

'Ready?' Lisa said.

Emily smiled. 'I have a name.'

'A name?'

'The couple at the other table.' She took a pen and a small notepad from her handbag, jotting down his name as she said it. 'Ben Stainton.'

Lisa threw open her arms. 'And?'

'I'm going to write a love story about Ben and his future wife.'

'Really? It'll be boring. They probably met in the dented tin aisle of Tesco.'

'Wow,' Emily said. 'What a start. Star-crossed lovers meet when they both reach for the same piece of salmon.'

'Reduced salmon.'

'Half of a salmon you mean?'

Lisa smiled and shook her head. 'Are we sharing a taxi?'

'Yeah.' Emily stood. 'Can you drop me off at the shops near my flat? I'm getting a bottle of wine.'

'Oh, you're so going to regret it in the morning.'

'Tomorrow is another day, Lisa. Tomorrow may never come.' She skipped her way towards the door.

SIX MONTHS LATER - Emily woke. The noise of the door to her flat closing, rousing her from her sleep. She turned onto her side, and stared blankly at her clothing from the night before strewn around the floor. She sighed deeply. Pulling her legs up to her waist she grasped her knees. Her one-night-stand from the previous evening hadn't even bothered to say goodbye. She was relieved about this though. Those awkward encounters which followed her drink-fuelled nights and ill-judged sexual liaisons. The morning shame she felt now stripped of the alcoholic veneer which covered the scrapes and scratches, bumps and bruises of her life. Searching for his name her head thumped as if resenting the unnecessary work involved, the usual painful penitence she paid for her excessive drinking. 'Was it Sean?' she muttered to herself. Closing her eyes as a lightning-strike of pain erupted in her temple. She couldn't remember. One seemed much like another. No. Sean was from last week. He was a brickie, she recollected that. The man from the night before, his name now agonisingly out of reach. What did it matter? He had served his purpose. A fit-looking younger man to share her bed with. Flopping down onto her back she stared at the ceiling. She could happily stay here all day, but her head ached. The paracetamols tantalisingly out of reach in the kitchen. Hungry as well, so, reluctantly Emily crawled out of bed, and aware of her nudity pulled on her dressing gown. The room stank. A left-over odour from the previous night pervaded the air. She opened the curtains and flung open the bedroom window. Ripping off the sheets from the bed, she marched through into the kitchen and threw them into the washing machine. Tramping into the bathroom she turned on the shower, allowing the water to reach the desired temperature. She gazed into the small bin by the side of the basin. A used condom lay on top. A visual reminder of what her life had now become. Staring at it for a moment she felt her cheeks burn as images from the previous night stood before her. She closed her eyes and brought a hand up to her mouth. Removing a black sack from under the sink she tipped the contents of the bin inside. Emily raced through the kitchen and outside, slamming the offending item into the wheelie bin. Returning to the bathroom, she showered before drying and dressing in jogging bottoms and a sweatshirt. As she pulled her damp hair into a ponytail, the doorbell sounded. She groaned and reluctantly trudged towards the door, opening it to a smiling Lisa.

Lisa stepped through the doorway and followed Emily into the lounge. 'Good night?'

Emily wandered over to the window and stared outside. 'Not bad.'

'Has he gone?'

She turned and slumped into a chair. 'Who?'

'Your one night stand.'

Emily focused on the floor. 'Yeah. Probably went home to his wife and kids.'

Lisa slipped onto a seat opposite and leant forward. 'I'm worried about you.'

Emily picked at a fingernail on her left hand with her right. 'Why? I'm ok.'

'How can you be ok, Emily? How many is that since Paul left?'

'I've stopped counting. What's the point? I'm just getting him out of my system that's all.'

Lisa turned away and dropped her head. 'People are talking.'

Emily crossed her arms glaring at Lisa. 'What people?'

Lisa fixed her friend with a stare and shrugged. 'Friends.'

She snorted. 'Friends. I don't tell anyone else how to live their life. I don't judge. People … friends … they can all piss-off!'

'It's been six months. You can't let your life drift by like this and—'

'Stop nagging.' She tapped her right foot. Her left leg sternly crossing her right. 'It's my life.'

'I know but—'

Emily picked up a nearby cushion and pulled it tight to her body. 'It's all right for you. With your four bedroomed house in suburbia. Two point four children and a perfect husband.'

Lisa half-smiled. 'I wouldn't call Tim perfect.'

Emily stood and wandered back to the window, staring into the street outside. 'It's my body. What's the matter, Lisa? Don't you like the idea of having a slapper for a friend?'

'Don't be silly. I never said—'

'I can't help who I am. Who I've become. If you're not happy with me, with us …'

'Look, Emily.' She stood and frowned. 'I want what's best for you. That's all.'

'Well stop talking to me as if I'm one of your pupils. I'm thirty-five, not fourteen. You always do it. You live your whole life as if it's inside a classroom. Sorry if I don't conform to your high morals. This isn't Holburn Grange Academy. If I want to sleep with five-hundred men, it's up to me. My choice, my ...' Her words faded into a whisper.

Lisa sighed. 'I'll put the kettle on shall I?' She moved towards Emily a little, but then stopped.

'Yeah. You do that.' Throwing the cushion on the settee.

Emily waited for Lisa to leave before turning. She paused, catching sight of herself in the mirror. The scowl on her face dissipating. Lifting a hand to her mouth, she winced as tears queued. Lisa's words resounded, a bell-like ring of truth that deafened her.

Lisa made tea and toast for the two of them. She placed the items on a tray and turned around as Emily entered.

Walking across to the window, Emily stopped. Her back to Lisa. 'I'm sorry, Lisa. It was out of order, what I said. I'm hungover, that's all.'

Lisa smiled, placing the tray down. 'Forget it. I didn't mean to lecture. Tim says I do it all the time.'

Emily turned, her eyes now red and puffy. 'I love you and Tim. It was unfair what I said. I ...' She lowered her head. 'Why do you tolerate me? When I'm always horrible to you.'

Lisa smiled. 'You're my best friend. The sister I never had.'

Emily's shoulders drooped as she brought her hands to her face. 'I don't deserve you.'

Lisa inched closer to Emily, her hand moving to finger her crucifix around her neck. 'When Mum died, you understood what I was going through. All the other girls at school didn't. You were there for me. You helped me through it. You were my rock.'

Emily half-smiled. 'Kindred spirits.'

'Yeah. You knew what I was going through. The others couldn't. I've never forgotten that.'

Emily turned and gazed outside into the backyard. 'I can't remember his name ... The guy from last night. I came back here and had sex with someone, and I can't even remember his name.' A loud sob escaped as Emily brought a hand to her mouth, too late.

Lisa strode across to Emily and hugged her. Pulling her friend tight into her body.

'I'm lost, Lisa. I'm lost, and I don't know how to find myself.' She buried her face on Lisa's shoulder.

'Oh, Emily.' Holding onto her friend, her sobbing now relentless.

Emily and Lisa entered the coffee shop. Emily headed to a vacant table near the window as Lisa ordered their drinks. She stared outside.

A couple stopped across the street at a bookshop. She watched as the man opened the door, the woman with the man kissed him on the lips as he turned to face her. Their faces seemed familiar. A recollection stirred somewhere deep within her mind. The dust from the memory, gently shaken from it. Where had she seen them? She mused.

Lisa arrived at the table. 'What are you looking at?' Severing any possible connection to the couple.

'Nothing really.' Turning back to face her friend. 'Looks like there's a bookshop opening over the road. I'll have to pop in there. They sell old books too.'

'A bookshop? That'll never work. Waterstones and Smiths will see to that.'

'I thought I knew the couple who opened the shop.'

Lisa placed the tray on the table. 'Oh yeah?' She pushed a cup and plate towards her friend. 'One Latte and I've got you a caramel shortcake.'

'I'm laying off the cakes. I'm getting a proper belly on me. Like a poisoned pup.' She patted her stomach.

Lisa grinned. 'Lovely turn of phrase.'

'My nan used to say it. Funny the things you remember.'

'So, do I have to eat both?'

Emily snatched one of the cakes. 'You just want me fat and frumpy. You're a feeder. I've read all about people like you.' Crumbs from the cake cascading onto the table as she bit into it.

'What should we do?' Lisa said. 'I've got a free day. Tim's looking after the kids, and I have my credit cards.'

'Shop?' Popping the last bit of cake into her mouth.

Lisa grinned. 'Why not.'

Lisa peered through the window of a boutique as Emily glanced across the road towards the bookshop.

Lisa clapped her hands together. 'I'm heading in.' Turning to face Emily. 'Tim's antennae will be twitching as we speak.'

'I'm going to look in the bookshop across the road,' Emily said.

'Ok. I'll meet you back here.'

Emily wandered across the street and looked through the window of the shop. The woman she'd seen earlier stood behind the counter. Where had she seen her before? Her face, and where they had met, agonisingly out of reach. She grasped the handle of the door and strolled in. The smell of new and old books hitting her immediately as she entered. The woman behind the counter smiled at her and Emily remembered. Of course, the restaurant. The couple on the table near to her and Lisa.

'I saw you open up,' Emily said. 'A new venture?'

'Just opened this week. A bit of a gamble, I know, but I've always wanted to run a bookshop.'

'So it's yours?'

The woman laughed. 'If you ignore the money we owe the bank. Anything in particular you're after?'

Emily slowly pirouetted taking in the shop's interior. 'I'm looking for poetry.'

The woman behind the counter came around and wandered towards one of the corners. 'Modern or classical?'

'Classical.'

'There are new books here.' Pointing at a shelf. 'If you want second-hand ones there are some over there.' Pointing at another.

Emily smiled. 'Thanks.' The woman returned to her previous place behind the counter.

Emily searched for several minutes before selecting a book. She leafed through the pages, stopping every now and then to read the verse. Satisfied, she made her way across to the counter.

'William Blake,' the woman said.

'What do you think?' Looking directly at her.

'Bit too religious for my tastes. All that Jerusalem and that. There's one of his I quite like though, how—'

'How sweet I roamed,' Emily said.

'Yeah.' Smiling at Emily. 'It has a particular resonance for me. £9.99, please.'

Emily held her credit card up to the machine. The machine beeped, signalling its approval. The woman popped the book and receipt into a small bag and handed it to her.

Emily smiled again. 'Thanks.' She turned, and headed for the door pausing briefly to glance around at the woman.

EMILY'S JOURNAL

May 14th, 2014 - *My most productive writing day to date. Six-thousand words! I contacted a friend of mine who still lives in London. She gave me the name and number of an agent that could be interested in my book. I've arranged a meeting with him.*

May 26th, 2014 – *Oliver has agreed to take me on. He seems very keen after reading the first three chapters of my book. We're meeting for lunch in Leeds next week. Maybe I will write a best-seller. Perhaps this is the opportunity I've been waiting for.*

June 2nd, 2014 – Met a man at a party. His name's Richard. Very handsome, intelligent and funny. He's been single for six months he told me. Asked for my number. I gave it to him. Perhaps it was the wine, or maybe he just picked the right time. I hope he phones.

I've started keeping a journal and decided the characters in my book would keep one too. It's a fabulous plot device for having their innermost feelings laid bare. Also, it feels cathartic for me. The maelstrom of thoughts swamping my mind are difficult to handle most days. Hopefully, this will help. I seem to have got to grips with my penchant for one-night stands. A thoroughly embarrassing episode if I'm honest. Losing Paul hit me harder than I imagined it would. Strange, the Emily who slept with all those men, and there were quite a few, doesn't feel like me. It's as if someone else lived out those months. Only if and when I meet that special person can I erase Paul entirely from my life. He still haunts me. My memories are replete with him. Pubs and restaurants, shops and theatres, and the flat. Even though I removed everything of his, his essence still pervades. Is this what people do? Pine for a relationship which hasn't existed for a long time. I spent yesterday mulling over what to do with the photos of us. Part of me wanted to burn them. Another part, cut him off the pictures. They are my life though. Paul was part of it for a long time. If I destroyed them, there would be no turning back. Maybe in the future, when the hurt has dissipated, I can gaze on them dispassionately. I finally decided to box them up and put them in the loft. If only all memories could be shelved so easily, and pushed into the dark corner of a dusty room.

I was surprised to receive a call from the man I met at a party. I'm going out for a meal with him tonight. This could be the first step towards forgetting Paul.

After showering and thinking about what to wear, I decided on a red dress. It's vital I make a good impression. Who knows, maybe I'll obtain some ideas for my book. I'll take a pad and pencil. Just in case.

CHAPTER TWO

AUGUST 2015 - Grace peered through the window of the shop at the expensive looking handbag resting on a shelf inside. Straining to see the price tag hanging from one of its handles, she huffed, the cost on the label beyond her vision. She would have to go inside and ask. She disliked doing this. The boutique smart and fashionable, she was sure the bag would be out of her price range. Did she want to endure the shock you sometimes experience when you find out the cost of something? She would never know if she didn't go in though. She could always mask her surprise if it was above her budget. Grace spun around startled by the sound of a horn. She glared at the offending vehicle, an impatient taxi driver, its passage blocked by a double-parked car. Then she spotted him. Was it Ben? Certain it was, Grace cupped a hand above her eyes to shield them from the sun. He was supposed to be away, out of town. That's what he'd told her. She edged closer, keeping people between herself and him. His gait so familiar to her now, any doubt it wasn't him evaporated. She watched as he disappeared from sight around a bend. She waited a few moments, considering her options, and then set off after him. He stood on a corner and hailed a taxi. Grace, realising she would lose him, desperately searched for one herself. Her eyes flicking from Ben, who was now getting into a car, back to the passing traffic. She clenched her jaw and brought her hands to her face watching helplessly as the vehicle carrying him, pulled away. A car drew up next to her and Grace turned. The window lowered, and as she dropped down to view the occupant, a smiling Lucy beamed back at her.

'I thought it was you,' Lucy said. 'Out shopping?'

Grace yanked open the door and jumped in. 'Thank God, Lucy. Follow that taxi.' Nodding in the direction it headed.

Lucy threw her head back and snorted. 'What?'

Grace put a hand on Lucy's arm. 'Please. I haven't time to explain. I need you to follow that car.'

Lucy narrowed her eyes. 'Yeah, ok.' Slamming the car into gear and heading after it.

Grace forced a smile and lowered her eyes. 'Sorry about this. Ben's in there.'

Lucy viewed her friends face. 'Why, what's up?'

'He told me he'd be away this weekend, but I've just spotted him in town.'

'Right. And you think?'

'I don't know what to think. It could be entirely innocent.'

'Of course. Ben may have changed his mind. Maybe—'

Grace shook her head. 'Why didn't he ring?'

'Have you called him?'

'I tried a couple of times this morning. His mobile is turned off. It keeps going to answerphone.'

Lucy accelerated. Two car lengths between hers and the taxi now as she continued to head away from the town.

Lucy glanced at her friend. 'You and Ben? I didn't know you were—'

Grace put a hand over her mouth briefly. 'It's complicated.'

Lucy half-smiled. 'You never said you and he were—'

Grace turned her head and gazed out of the passenger window. 'It's a long story.'

Lucy glanced at Grace again. 'Right. I didn't know. We seldom talk these days.'

'Grace continued to stare outside. 'I was going to, I …'

Lucy patted her friend on her knee. 'Forget it. You can tell me later.'

She turned to face Lucy and forced a smile. 'Thanks.'

'He's heading towards Marton by the look of it.'

Grace nodded. 'His flat.'

The car turned onto Cypress Road no more than fifty metres behind the taxi. Lucy's eyes darted from her friend and then back to the road. 'Shall I catch them up?'

Grace unbuckled her seatbelt. 'No. Can you stop? I'll walk from here.'

The car glided to a halt at a bus stop.

Grace opened the door, and Lucy took hold of her arm. 'Is everything all right, Grace?'

She turned and kissed her friend's cheek. 'It's fine. Thanks for the lift. I owe you one.' She jumped out of the car and closed the door.

Lucy lowered the window. 'I'll ring later shall I?'

Grace stopped and forced another smile as she waved half-heartedly at her friend. She watched as Lucy turned her car around and drove off. Throwing her bag across her shoulder, she marched in the direction of Ben's flat. Ben's now empty taxi passed her as she strode along the pavement. She stopped at the end of the road. His flat in clear view, simultaneously repelling and drawing her on. Taking out her mobile she rang his number again. It went straight to the answer-phone. Grace tossed it into her bag. She edged closer to the property and slumped on a wall outside considering her options. Thoughts swirled in her mind. A long five minutes limped past. She stood, blew out hard and headed for the flat. She stopped outside the front door and stared at the upstairs window. What if he was with someone, she thought. How stupid, how silly she would feel. They weren't a couple, not a proper one anyway. He'd made no promises to her and yet the jealousy she felt drenched her. Her hand hovered above the bell. She could go, and he would be none the wiser. Walk away as if this never happened. How foolish of her to follow him here. It was his life, none of her business. Grace glanced up at the window half-expecting to see a smiling Ben waving down at her. Nothing stirred. Grace, her heart pumping, her breaths increasing, put her hand on the cold metal of the door handle and turned it. Surprisingly it opened. She peeked through the small opening and up the flight of stairs to his flat. She wanted to call, but the words she wanted to say stalled in her throat. Tears appeared from nowhere and tumbled down her cheeks. She wiped her face, shaking her head at her emotional stupidity. Slowly, sheepishly, she climbed the stairs. Every successive creak of her footfalls on the steps amplified in the eerie quietness. She paused and listened for the slightest noise above. The silence mocked her. Arriving at the top, she reached for the handle and pushed open the door to his flat. The hushed stillness inside deafened her. She expected voices, laughter, or … she pushed the thought away. The entrance to the living room and to the kitchen, both lay open. Both empty. Only the bathroom and bedroom remained. She nudged open the bathroom door, the creaking of the hinges causing her to catch her breath. It too was empty. Grace stared at the last remaining door. Her heartbeat now banging inside her chest. She wanted to go, terrified by what she would find behind the door. But she couldn't. She needed to know. Hesitatingly she tiptoed forward and stopped. She held her breath and placed a trembling hand on the doorknob. She paused and gasped for rarefied air, briefly closing her eyes. Slowly she turned the handle and pushed it open.

THREE MONTHS EARLIER - Grace turned onto the side street and headed along it. About halfway down she saw the shop. A large sign in the shape of a book hung from the building above the window. She stopped and peered through the glass. He stood behind the counter talking to a customer, Grace presumed. She waited outside until he'd finished serving and as the man left she ventured in. Ben peered up from his counter and smiled pleasantly at her.

Grace smiled back and edged towards him, stopping in front of the counter. 'Mr Stainton?'

His eyes crinkled at the corners, a smile spreading across his face. 'Ben. Call me Ben. Hardly anyone calls me Mr Stainton. It makes me sound like a bank manager.'

Grace smiled again. 'Hi, Ben. I've come about the job. We spoke on the phone. Grace Newton.'

Ben closed the till giving her his full attention. He held out a hand, and Grace shook it. 'Yes. I remember,' he said.

'Are you still looking for someone?'

'I am. Do you have a CV, Grace?'

'Of course.' Removing an A4 size envelope from her bag, she handed it to him.

He pulled a piece of paper from it and fixed his eyes on her. 'Would you like a tea or coffee?'

'I'm all right thanks.'

'I'll have a gander at this.' He held up the paper. 'Why don't you look around the shop while I do?' He smiled again.

Grace nodded. Pulling herself away from his sapphire eyes, she moved from the counter into one of the corners. Ben leant back on a stool with the piece of paper in his hand and began reading it. She watched him through a gap in one of the shelves. He was as handsome as she remembered. He ran his hand through his hair, pushing it into something resembling order. What was he thinking? He put his hand on his chin, stroking the stubble with his thumb and index finger. Ben looked up. Grace quickly averted her gaze.

'It's impressive,' he said.

She stepped out from behind the shelving. 'Thank you.'

'Aren't you a little overqualified to work in a bookshop? I'm not paying much more than the minimum wage.'

She strolled back towards the counter. 'The money's unimportant.'

He glanced at the sheet of paper again. 'A degree in English-language?'

'Yes. I do a bit of writing. It pays ok. But I love books. Where better to work. If you love books, I mean.'

He smiled at her. 'I see.' Grace studied his face carefully. Ben met her gaze. 'It's only two or three days a week to start with, although it could be more.'

'That's fine. As I said, the money's irrelevant.'

'Well.' He offered his hand. 'The job's yours, if you want it.'

'Thanks.' Grace bent forward and shook it.

He smiled again and placed Grace's CV on the counter. 'What about that drink?'

'I'd love one … Ben.'

She watched as he disappeared into the rear of the shop. 'Tea or coffee?' he shouted.

'Coffee, please. Milk, no sugar.'

After drinking the tea and chatting pleasantly for an hour, Grace left. Ben had taken her mobile number, informing her he would ring the next day to let her know when she could start. She headed home, the beating in her chest reaching its usual rhythm. Collecting a meal for one and a bottle of wine en route, she finally arrived at her flat. Grace pushed open the door, tossed the car keys onto the telephone table, and stooped to pick up the post from the floor as she entered.

She sat at the table with the meal she had warmed in the microwave and a large glass of wine. Mouthfuls of food punctuated by gulps of her drink. After eating, she deposited the plate in the dishwasher, tipped the remainder of the alcohol into her glass and took a large swig.

She spotted the book resting on the table near to her, its cover battered and worn. She downed the rest of her drink and shakily placed the glass down. Her hand hovered above the book briefly before opening it. Inside, written in bold handwriting on the first page, *this journal belongs to Sarah Williams.* Grace brought her hands up to her face and covered her eyes. An idea formed in her mind. She stood, moved across to the dresser and rifled through the drawers, receipts and papers pushed aside. A red book with her name stencilled on the front lay in one of the corners. She snatched up the book, returned to her seat, and opened the first page. She began to write.

May 28th, 2015. – I met Ben today for the first time. He's incredibly handsome. Even more so than I remember. I can understand why Sarah fell for him.

She paused and tapped the pen on the table.

Is what I'm doing so wrong? Maybe only time can be the judge and jury.

THE NEXT WEEK - Grace entered the shop carrying two coffees. Ben, who was already there, lifted his head and smiled. 'Morning.' Grace held up the drinks. 'I've brought us coffee. No offence, but that instant stuff of yours is horrible.'

Ben smiled and nodded knowingly. 'Sarah always said that. She would only drink decent coffee. Detested instant. Said it was an insult to her taste buds.'

'Sarah?' Grace forced herself to meet his stare.

Ben's smile fell from his face. 'My wife.'

Grace stared downwards, her resolve weakening. 'I didn't know you're married.' Raising her head slightly, she handed him a coffee.

'She died.'

Grace briefly closed her eyes as guilt swamped her. A lump appeared in her throat from nowhere. She swallowed hard. 'Oh, Ben. I'm sorry. I didn't mean to—'

'You didn't know. It happened a few months ago.'

She shifted awkwardly. Ben's candidness taking her by surprise. He dropped his eyes down and shut the till drawer. 'Are you ready for your first full day?'

She smiled. 'I am.' As if the conversation had not taken place.

'Well. Come around here, and I'll show you how this thing works. It's a little temperamental.'

Grace smiled and joined him next to the till. 'It's been a long time since I operated one of these. It takes me back to my student days.'

Ben gave Grace a run-down of what was involved in the running of the shop. After teaching her how to operate the till, and how to scan the barcodes of new books into it, she felt confident. Ben left late morning leaving her in the shop. Customers were few and far between. Grace filled the time by rearranging books on shelves and performing a general tidy up. Ben wasn't the most organised of people, understandable after his loss, she reasoned. By late afternoon she had managed to get the shop in a much tidier state.

She sat with a book in front of her, and glancing up at the clock, stopped reading and closed it as Lucy entered.

Lucy strolled across to the counter and stood in front of her friend. 'So, this is your life now?'

'How did you—'

'Sally Adams. I ran into her earlier. She said she saw you through the window in here.'

Grace held up a hand, looked away and began tidying up the counter. 'I know what you're going to say.'

'You do?'

'It's hard to explain, Lucy.'

'Try me.'

'I can't leave Ben on his own after what I did. You must see that?'

'That's exactly what you should do. The man's life has been turned upside down by the loss of his wife. What do you think this will achieve?'

Grace turned away from her friend. 'I don't know. It's just something I have to do.'

Lucy slowly shook her head. 'What if he found out about your connection with his wife?'

'Sarah,' Grace said. 'That was her name. *Sarah.*' And spun around to face her friend.

Lucy stepped to the side of the counter and studied Grace, slightly tilting her head. 'I'm sorry. Sarah. What will he think—'

'I don't know. I couldn't, I mean, I can't just sit back and watch him suffer. Maybe I can console him. Maybe—'

'This will end poorly, Grace. I'm your best friend. I can't allow you to continue to beat yourself up over something that was an accident. A random convergence of events. That's all it was.'

'I needed a job. You know I love books. Where better than this place.'

Lucy folded her arms. 'You don't expect me to believe that do you?'

Grace shrugged. 'I don't care.' She reached into her pocket and pulled out a tissue.

'What about the creative writing course?'

'I packed it in. I couldn't go back there. The memories ...' Looking towards the ceiling Grace blew out.

The door to the shop opened, and Ben sauntered in carrying two coffees. 'I've got you a latte.' Holding it aloft.

Grace turned and forced a smile. 'Thanks.'

He lowered his eyes at Grace. 'You ok?' Ben glanced at Lucy and popped Grace's coffee down.

'I'll give you a call in the week,' Lucy said. 'We'll meet for a coffee.'

Grace nodded. 'Yeah, absolutely.' Pushing the tissue into her jeans. She glanced at Ben. 'This is a good friend of mine, Ben. Lucy.'

Lucy smiled as Ben strolled across and shook her hand. 'Lucy. Nice to meet you.'

'Likewise.' Smiling at Ben, she turned to face Grace. 'See you later. Don't forget that coffee.'

Grace nodded. 'I'll phone.'

Lucy nodded back, smiled at Ben and left.

Ben eyed Grace and moved nearer. 'Are you sure you're all right?'

Grace half-smiled. 'Lucy was telling me about an old friend of ours who died, that's all. A bit of a shock.'

'Oh, I'm sorry to hear that.'

She picked up her coffee and waved at him with her other hand. 'Forget it. Tell me about your day.'

CHAPTER THREE

JUNE 2014 - Emily stood outside the restaurant and viewed her reflection in the window. Moving her head first right, and then left, she brushed the front of her dress. Doubts crept into her mind. Did she look ok? She now wished she had put on the black dress instead of the red one she wore.

She groaned loudly. 'For Christ sake, Emily. Get a grip of yourself.' A woman passing by glanced across at her before continuing on.

'This time last month,' Emily whispered. 'You were picking men up and taking them back to your flat, for ...' She closed her eyes and blushed at the thought. *It's a date, that's all. He'll love you. He'll hate you,* said her inner voice. If only she had put on the black dress. This red one made her look cheap. Would he think? Would he expect? That wasn't in her plan. A pleasant meal with an attractive man, that's all tonight was. 'You look fine,' she said to herself. 'For your age.' Emily studied her watch. Already ten minutes late. She couldn't go home and change, it would take too long. She huffed, turned to face the door, and entered.

The waiter showed her across the room to a table against the far wall.

Richard stood as she approached, smiling at her. 'I didn't know what drink to get you. I ordered a bottle of white ... If that's ok?'

She returned his smile and planted herself opposite. 'White's good.' In truth, anything alcoholic would have done. 'Sorry I'm late.'

'It's a woman's prerogative.'

'I suppose it is.' Picking up her glass she took a sip.

He was as handsome as she'd remembered him from their meeting at the party. She had drunk a significant amount that night and couldn't remember much of the evening. What bit she did remember though, was that she had given her number to a guy called Richard. She never actually thought he would phone. Men who asked for her number didn't always. She put this down to male bravado. When the beer was in some were full of themselves, but when they'd sobered up they thought better of it. Certainly the ones with wives or girlfriends.

She intended going steady tonight, making a solemn promise to herself. No steaming-drunk, first date sex for him. She planned on being elusive for a change.

Richard handed her one of the menus. 'The waiter said there are specials as well. On the board over there.' Nodding at the wall behind her.

Emily accepted the menu from him. 'I'm sure I can find something in here. A friend of mine in London worked at a swanky restaurant. She told me the specials were usually stuff they wanted rid of.'

'You worked in London?'

'Ten years of commuting.'

'Ever thought of moving there, permanently?'

'Absolutely not,' she said.

Richard smiled. 'Why? Don't you like the big city?'

'Too hectic. The people are ignorant as well. I prefer it up north, where genuine people live.'

'You don't work there now, then?'

Emily threw her head back and giggled. 'Packed my job in. I worked in a publishing house, and the drip, drip, drip of travelling up and down the country turned into a deluge one day. I marched into my boss's office and handed in my notice. She was shocked I remember. Quite enjoyed that.'

'Didn't you like the job?'

'Yeah. Sort of. I didn't hate it. Loved the money.'

Richard nodded. 'Publishers. Any bestsellers I might know?'

'We published non-fiction. A lot of academic books, that sort of thing. You may have seen the classic. *Animal husbandry and the pitfalls.*'

Richard chuckled. 'I think I missed that particular gem.' Gently tapping her hand. 'What do you do now?'

'Nothing.'

'Nothing?'

Emily leant back in her chair and took a large gulp of wine. 'Yeah. Indolence makes a fabulous pair of slippers.'

'I wish I could afford to do that. I sell cars for a living. Admittedly, top of the range, expensive cars.'

Emily smiled. 'I can't afford to not work. Well, not forever. My savings will run out eventually. I am writing a book though.'

'A follow-up to Animal husbandry?'

'No.' She giggled. 'If I ever manage to finish it.'

Richard smiled at her. 'I'm sure you will.'

'How do you know? We've only just met.'

'I have a feel for these things. You seem the determined sort.'

'I've got a contingency plan. In case I don't manage to get it published.'

'What's that then?' A waitress appeared next to them, pen poised.

They both ordered starters and main courses. The waitress smiled politely, collected the menus, and left.

Richard sipped his drink and picked up the wine bottle. He paused, gazed at her, and replenished their glasses. 'Come on then. What's your contingency plan?'

'Marry a rich man and live off him.'

Richard raised his glass aloft. 'Gooood plan.'

Emily leant back in her seat. 'What about your job?'

'It isn't what I had in mind when I left school. But after being tossed about like flotsam on the sea of life, you find yourself washed up on a beach somewhere. A beach called reality.'

'Love your metaphor.' She removed a small notepad from her handbag. 'You don't mind if I nick it do you?' She jotted it down.

Richard furrowed his brow. 'Why?'

'For my story. I'm always on the look-out for bits of dialogue. That sounded great.'

Richard raised his eyebrows. 'Would I make a good character?' He took a sizable mouthful from his glass.

Emily smiled and leant in closer. 'I see you in a puffy shirt and breeches. Not sure if you'd be a hero or a villain yet.'

'Hero, definitely.'

'Actually, it's a love story.' Sidestepping his comment.

'Love story, eh. What's it about?'

'A couple called Ben and ... I haven't decided on a name for his wife yet.'

'Will that be enough to make a full book?'

'There'll be a bit more to it than that. I've only just started it really. You can read it when I finish it.'

'I will. I'll look forward to that.'

Emily picked up her glass and took a small sip. 'Why don't you pack your job in?'

'Not everyone's as—'

'Mad?' Emily said.

'I was going to say ... brave.'

'Oh, I am. Brave that is. I'm Boudicca, Queen of the Iceni, until my credit card bill pops through the door.'

Richard laughed. 'My bill generally resembles the battle of the Somme.'

'Oh dear. Sounds like you need to find yourself a wealthy widow.'

'Mmm. Not a bad shout. However, I was thinking more along the line of my own dealership.'

Emily raised her glass. 'That works too. Here's to your first million.'

Richard raised his glass, clinking it with Emily's. 'I'll drink to that.'

They ate their meal and chatted some more. Emily increasingly charmed by her companion. He seemed to like her company too. After paying their bill – Emily insisting on paying half – they found themselves in the street, amid a throng of Thursday night revellers.

'Where did you say you live?' Richard asked.

Emily fished in her bag. 'Nunthorpe.' Pulling her phone out she searched for a number.

Richard edged a little closer. 'I can drop you off on my way home. I don't mind.'

'I thought you told me you lived in Darlington?'

'I did. I do,' Richard said. 'I don't mind dropping you off, though. Make sure you reach home safely.'

Emily considered this for a moment. Maybe Richard was merely being gallant. Or was he expecting something other than the sticky toffee pudding for afters? She couldn't tell. 'That would be stupid. It's miles out of your way.'

'At least let me call you a taxi?'

Emily smiled at him. 'A friend's picking me up. You phone one for yourself.'

'If you're sure?'

'I am.'

Richard phoned for a taxi and peered back at Emily. He half-smiled and shuffled his feet. 'Would you like to do this again? Or something a bit more exciting?'

Emily caught a hint of desperation in his voice. 'What did you have in mind, *Mr Car salesman.*' Sensing she now held the upper hand. He likes me, she thought.

'Have you been to the races?'

'Horseracing?'

'Yeah. I've a couple of tickets for York on Saturday. A friend of a friend owns a nag. We could make a day of it … or a weekend?'

Emily leant in closer, lowering her voice. 'Stay over?'

'Single rooms … I don't want you to think …'

Emily put a hand on his arm. 'I was hoping for the bridal suite.'

Richard grinned. He turned square on and stared into her eyes. 'I really enjoyed tonight.'

'I did too.' Her jocular countenance shelved for the moment. The kiss, when it came was functional. A small peck on either cheek. A taxi pulled up next to them.

Richard motioned behind him. 'My carriage. Are you sure you'll be all right?' Turning, he opened the passenger door.

'Fine. She's on her way now.' She held up her phone. Richard jumped in. Emily watched as the car drew away and disappeared out of sight. Searching for the number of the taxi firm she generally used, Emily dialled. She paused and felt a presence next to her. Looking up from her phone she stared into the face of someone. Someone she would rather not be staring at.

'Emily. I thought it was you.' The man rocked from side to side as if standing on a trampoline. His words heavily slurred.

She scrutinised the familiar-looking man but couldn't put a name to his face at first. Blushing when she realised it was one of the many men she had taken home.

'I'm sorry ...'

'Don't say you've forgotten my name.' He moved closer to her. Too close. His alcohol filled breath causing her to recoil. Backing away she realised she now stood on the edge of the pavement, rapidly running out of space she stopped.

'You screamed it enough when we were shagging.' Emily's face blushed further as a couple, passing by, stared at the pair of them. The woman, Emily realised, instantly weighing up her character.

'Andy.' Remembering his name. Attempting to edge sideways and gently push him away. 'I'm on my way home.'

He laughed loudly. 'Why don't I come back with you? Make a night of it?'

She edged further to the side and raced along Linthorpe Road, towards town. Andy tottering after her. 'My friends picking me up,' she said.

'I don't mind.' Catching her up. 'Invite your friend along. I'm a man of the world. More's the merrier.'

'You're married.' Quickening her step in an attempt to put distance between them. 'If I remember rightly.'

'That didn't stop you last time.' He grabbed her arm and pulled her closer. Emily wrestled free and jogged across Borough Road with the man still in pursuit.

'What the hell's up with you. You lead a man on ...'

She hurried along the pavement and turned right onto Baker Street. Checking over her shoulder, she could see the man stumbling along after her. 'You're a cock tease,' he said.

Fighting to keep the distance between them, she stumbled and dropped her handbag. Her heart a jackhammer, pounding against her chest. She bent to retrieve it as he caught her up and gripped hold of her again. Emily struggled to break free from his grasp and stumbled backwards into a parked car.

Someone grabbed hold of Andy and pushed him forcefully in the chest. Andy, unable to keep his balance, fell in a heap. He looked up at the huge person glaring down at him.

'The lady wants you to leave her alone,' the man said. 'Now piss off!'

Andy clambered to his feet and careered into a large plastic bin. He recovered and stumbled on, turning left back onto Linthorpe Road in a drunken, wide arc.

The man turned to face Emily. 'Are you ok?'

'Yeah,' she said. Staring at him she studied his familiar face, and as the memory arrived, she smiled at him. 'Did you marry?'

He furrowed his brow. 'Sorry?'

'I was in the restaurant ... When you proposed.'

He brought a hand to his mouth. 'Oh, my God. How embarrassing was that?'

Emily smiled. 'I thought it was romantic.'

'Yes. We married.' Holding out his hand. 'Ben.'

She scanned about as she shook it. 'Emily ... Your wife. Is she with you?'

'No. Sarah's at home. I've been for a couple of pints with some mates. Come in here.' Ushering her towards the pub doorway, she followed him inside.

'I'll get you a taxi. In case any more nutters are about.'

'It's fine.' Emily said. 'My friend's picking me up.'

'Are you sure?'

'Absolutely.'

Ben held out a hand again. She shook it. 'Wait until I tell Sarah I ran into someone who saw me propose. She still teases me about it now.'

'Can I buy you a drink as a thank you?' she said.

'Thanks for the offer but I really need to go home. Gene.' Ben made eye contact with the barman. 'Look after this young lady until her lift comes, will you?'

'Of course.' In a camp timbre.

'Thanks, again,' Emily said. Ben smiled pleasantly and then he was gone.

'Would you like a drink?' Gene asked.

She turned and ambled towards the bar. 'A glass of white wine, please.'

'Pinot Grigio ok, honey?'

'Pinot Grigio's fine.' She hopped onto a stool at the end of the counter, pulled out her notebook and jotted something inside.

Gene placed the glass in front of Emily. 'Is Ben a friend of yours then?'

Emily pulled out a note and handed it to him. 'One for yourself. No. He saved me from a drunken yob.'

'Thanks, beautiful.' Taking the note from her, he handed Emily her change. Reaching behind him he rang a bell, the customers in the room turning and cheering as he did.

'See.' Looking towards the people now staring at him. 'Not everyone's as greedy as you buggers.'

Emily turned her head away, her cheeks glowing.

Gene leant across the bar, lowering his voice. 'He's wonderful, our Ben. Only likes women, unfortunately. Sarah's a lucky cow.'

'Does he come in here often?'

Gene gently tapped her arm. 'Every week. Ben and a couple of his friends usually, but sometimes with his wife. Don't be getting any ideas though. He's happily married.'

'I wasn't.' Crossing her heart. 'I'm a writer.' Gene narrowed his eyes and shrugged. Emily continued. 'I'm always on the lookout for interesting characters to incorporate into my book. Someone with that special trait.' Emily winked. 'Someone mysterious or exciting.'

Gene leant forward on his elbows. 'Wouldn't that be wrong? Using real people.'

'It's not as clear-cut as that. By the time I've fleshed them out. Changed their names, lives, no-one will recognise them.'

'I see,' he said. And pulled a pint for a regular who now stood at the bar.

'For example.' Taking a sip of her drink. 'What does Ben do for a living?'

'He's a carpenter.'

'Well,' she said. Putting down her glass. 'My character might be a plumber. Ben's got light-brown hair. My character could be blonde.'

'Oh,' Gene clapped. 'Blondes are my favourite. What would my character be like?'

Emily waved him closer. 'A six-foot-six rugby player.'

'You're pulling my leg,' he said. Tapping Emily on her arm again.

She picked up her glass. 'Tell me more about Ben and his wife, Sarah.'

'Well …' Gene began.

The taxi pulled up outside of Emily's flat. After paying the driver, she sauntered inside. Pulling her notebook out and tossing her handbag on the settee, she opened a drawer and removed a small exercise book. Written on the front, in her handwriting, the words – *Notes for my novel*. Below this: *Working title*: and a question mark. She opened the book at the first page, stopping at the name she had written down months earlier – *Ben Stainton*. Next to this another question mark. She crossed this out and wrote: *Sarah Stainton*. Then, from Ben's name, she drew an arrow pointing down. Under this, she wrote: *Carpenter*. She continued to add the information she had wheedled out of Gene while waiting for her taxi. After filling several pages, Emily closed both books and smiled to herself. Depositing the notebook back in her handbag and the larger book in the drawer, she turned off the light and headed to bed.

Had a terrific night, apart from meeting one of my one-night stands. I was mortified. Why is this? It's my body, I can do what I want with it. If I sleep with men, it's no one's business but mine. Why is there one rule for men and another for women? Men who sleep around are revered. Jack-the-lad types. Players. Women are treated differently. We can fool ourselves it doesn't matter, but it does. We're slags. Easy lays. Gagging for it. That's the trouble with reputations. Easy to acquire, difficult to shake. Hopefully, I won't run into any more of those best-forgotten memories.

Richard's interesting. I already love his sense of humour. It's similar to mine. He's handsome, but then I probably wouldn't have agreed to a date if he wasn't. Am I really so shallow? It's early days yet, but he looks promising. He's passed the first test though. Lisa will be around tomorrow. She'll want a blow by blow account of my evening. I've decided to tease her a little and make her wait. Why should I give up my life so easily? If she wants to know, she'll have to work for it.

Got some exciting stuff for my book. A story's forming. I'm going to write a complete outline. Work out the characters and where they're heading. After writing the initial chapters, I'd stalled a little. But I have some thrilling ideas bubbling in my head.

CHAPTER FOUR

Emily sat at the table in her kitchen, sipping her freshly made coffee. She smiled upon hearing a knock on the door. The rat-tat, rat-tat, familiar calling card of Lisa.

'It's open,' she shouted

Lisa bounded in. 'Morning.' A grin spread across her face.

Emily stood and plucked the newspaper from the table. 'Get yourself a cup of coffee.' Sitting back in her chair she raised the paper, deliberately holding it in front of herself, awaiting the inevitable grilling she was about to receive.

Lisa poured herself a coffee from the cafetiere and nestled onto a seat opposite her friend. She pulled down the paper in front of Emily. 'Well?' Throwing her arms open. 'How did it go?'

Emily smiled and folded the paper. 'Great.' She took a sip of coffee. 'He seems nice.'

Lisa pouted. 'Nice?'

'Ok, he's handsome and funny.'

'You didn't …?'

'No I didn't. We had our meal, and he jumped in a taxi.'

'Are you meeting again?'

Emily drained her cup, plonking it on the table. 'York races.'

'York races?'

'Yeah.' Smiling at her friend.

Lisa rolled her eyes. 'Christ, Emily. This is like pulling teeth.'

'He asked me if I fancied going to York races with him. We may even make a weekend of it. That's everything.'

Lisa winked. 'A dirty weekend?'

Emily stood and carried her cup across to the sink. 'Do you recall the couple at Savino's? When the man proposed to the woman?'

'Vaguely. What about them?'

'I ran into him last night. He saved me from an amorous drunk.'

'This was obviously after Richard left?'

'It was.'

Lisa narrowed her eyes. 'Who was the drunk?'

'I don't know.' Turning away from her friend she waved her hand. 'Just some yob. They married.'

'Who?'

Emily sighed. 'The guy who proposed to the woman. Ben Stainton. That's his name. His wife's called Sarah.'

Lisa glanced upwards. 'Wonderful. I'm more interested in Richard.'

'I've told you everything. When I have more to tell, after the races, I'll let you know. Don't worry you'll get the full blow by blow account.'

Lisa raised her eyebrows. 'Blow by blow. That—'

Emily smiled and pointed at her friend. 'Stop that, Lisa.' Who comically lowered her eyebrows.'

Emily turned and picked up her exercise book, holding it up. 'Do you remember the story I'm writing? The love story?'

Lisa sighed. 'Again, vaguely. I thought you'd given up on that.'

'No. I haven't written much for a while. But I've decided to give it another go. Oliver phoned and asked how it was going.'

'What did you say?'

'I lied. I told him I've written another three chapters. He wants an outline of my story.'

'It's a huge undertaking. Especially with a man on the scene.'

'Well …' Turning to face her friend. 'I've decided to tell their story.'

'And how will you manage that? You don't even know them.'

'I have a plan.' She smiled at Lisa. 'I've a little background stuff, and I'll be creative with the rest. It will be a *story,* I'm not going to merely recount their life.'

Lisa drained her cup. 'Well. Good luck with that. When am I going to meet this Richard then?'

'It's early days, Lisa. I don't want to scare him off.'

Lisa opened her mouth. 'Cheeky cow.'

Emily held up the pot. 'Another coffee?'

ONE MONTH LATER – Emily checked her appearance for the umpteenth time in the mirror, glanced at her watch, and sighed. Why was she nervous? This job, and getting it, wasn't the end of the world. The money would come in useful of course. The novelty of not working had somewhat worn off as well. She really needed more structure in her life. Something to fill the long days. Her book had progressed quickly in the early stages, but now she had reached an impasse. If she couldn't finish it, let alone get it published, she would need to work eventually. Her savings rapidly diminishing. Blowing out hard, she gave her head a metaphorical shake and entered the building. Following the directions in the letter in her hand, Emily made her way to the reception, stopping at a large desk.

The young woman seated behind it lifted her head and smiled pleasantly as Emily held out the piece of paper. 'I'm here for an interview.'

The woman took it from her and read it. 'If you'd like to take a seat.' Emily thanked her and positioned herself in a chair close by. She watched as the woman held a brief conversation on the phone.

'Someone will be along soon,' the receptionist said. 'Can I get you a drink?'

'I'm fine, thanks.' The woman nodded at her and resumed her typing.

Emily rechecked her phone, and turned it off as a second woman approached her. 'Emily?' Offering her hand, she introduced herself.

Emily smiled. 'Yes.' Shaking it warmly.

'If you'd like to come with me?'

She followed the woman through a maze of corridors, eventually stopping outside a door. The woman knocked, a voice from within inviting her inside.

'Emily Kirkby,' the woman said to the two people seated behind the desk, a middle-aged man and a slightly younger woman.

The man gestured towards a chair in front of them. 'Take a seat, Emily.' The woman who'd shown Emily into the room nodded at the three of them and left.

The man held out his hand. 'I'm Paul, and this is my colleague, Jane.' Emily exchanged handshakes with the pair.

'Let me tell you about the job,' he said. 'We're looking for someone to establish and run a creative writing course. It's something the University has considered for some time.' He folded his hands and smiled at her.

The woman opened a file in front of her, pulling out a CV. 'There will be a qualification at the end of the course, but what we're looking for is someone who can bring something of themselves to it.'

Emily forced a smile. 'That'll be me.'

'I thought you'd say that,' Jane said. 'When can you start?'

'Are you serious?'

Jane nodded. 'We are.'

'Absolutely,' Paul said.

'You're the standout candidate.' Jane said. 'We obtained some impressive references. This meeting's just a formality. To confirm our gut instincts.'

Emily grinned. 'Anytime. That's the shortest interview I've ever had.'

The woman stood and pointed towards the door. 'Right. Let me show you around then.'

Emily bounded out of the University and pulled out her mobile. Finding his name, she phoned.

'Hi, gorgeous,' Richard said. 'Good news?'

'It is. You've had a reprieve. I've been offered the job so, I won't have to seek out a rich guy to live off.'

'Great. I was wondering if I should re-join that dating site. Will there be a celebratory drink?'

'Hell, yeah! My treat. Meet me at mine tonight, around 07:30. We'll go for a meal.'

'Yes, Madam. Anything else?'

'Yeah,' Emily said. 'Don't forget your toothbrush. You'll need it in the morning, handsome.'

Emily leant across and placed a hand on Richard's chest. He turned his head towards her and opened an eye.

'Good night?' Emily said.

'Wasn't bad. The meal and wine ...' Gazing upwards. '... fantastic. Especially the starter.'

'Nothing else?' Moving onto her side, her back to him.

'Did I tell you I spent the night with this gorgeous, intelligent woman.' Spooning her.

She scoffed. 'Clearly, she wasn't as wonderful as the Dublin-bay prawns.'

Richard chuckled. 'A good deal cheaper.'

She sniggered. 'It's a good job I don't offend easily.'

'Love your perfume.' Sniffing the nape of her neck, he gently kissed it. 'What is it?'

'Is this your attempt at seduction?'

'Is it working?'

She turned to face him. 'Needs a bit of tuition if you ask me.'

Richard winked. 'It worked last night.'

'Last night I was drunk. You will have to try a good deal harder.'

'Is that a pun?'

Emily ignored his remark and turned back onto her side. 'What are you up to today? And does it include me?'

Richard put his hands behind his head. 'How about we go away to an enchanting, country hotel? With stunning, Georgian architecture, and sumptuous, en-suite rooms. Award-winning food. All set within a magnificent location, surrounded by breathtaking gardens, and amazing views?'

She turned to face him again. 'Are you making this up?' Edging closer to him, she gazed into his eyes.

'No. I found it on the internet last night while you were brushing your teeth, or whatever women spend ages in the bathroom doing.' He held out his mobile. A picture of the hotel on the screen. 'Well? What do you think, gorgeous?'

Emily threw open her arms and lay back. 'Ok, Mr Darcy. You may ravish me, now.'

Richard leant across and kissed her on the lips. He winked. 'In vain have I struggled. It will not do. My feelings will not be repressed. You must allow me to tell you how ardently I admire and love you.'

Emily laughed. 'How long did it take you to learn that?'

'Long enough. I played the role at college. I was trying to impress a girl.'

'Did it work?'

'Nope,' he said. 'She married a mate of mine.'

'Can't remember the line. It's been ages since I read that book.' She laughed again. 'Have you any more?'

'Maybe later.' And kissed her passionately.

AUGUST 2014 - Richard stood at the bar getting served when Emily's phone sounded.

'Hi, Oliver,' Emily said.

'Good news. I've spoken with *Sanderson Publishers*. Do you know them?'

'Yeah. A friend of mine worked there.'

'I sent them the first three chapters of your book and the synopsis you emailed me. They're keen. They published that best-seller of Audrey Sampson—'

'Crossed paths?' Emily said.

'That's the one. They believe yours is very like it. They're particularly interested in books of a similar genre. Yours fits the bill.'

'High praise indeed.'

'How's it going?'

'Emily rubbed the back of her neck, glancing at Richard. 'Very well.'

'They've offered an advance,' Oliver said.

'You're kidding?'

'No. £50,000. I'm a fabulous agent. I told them others were interested. Laid it on thick and they took the bait.'

She puffed out her cheeks. '£50,000?'

Richard returned with the drinks and sat next to Emily, pushing a glass towards her.

Emily, the phone still pressed to her ear, mouthed a thank you.

Oliver chuckled. 'It's very unusual for this to happen. I'm sure you know that. Especially for a first-time writer. I've told them you'll need six to eight months to finish the first draft. They seem happy with that.

'Six to eight months?'

'Are you ok with the timescale?' Oliver said.

'Yeah, absolutely.'

'Good. Don't forget to send me the next few chapters. I'm keen to read them myself.'

'I will.'

'Who was that?' Richard said.

'Oliver.'

'Good news?'

'Good and bad. He's had interest from a publisher, and they've offered me an advance.'

'How much?'

Emily smiled. '£50,000.'

Richard whistled. 'I wish I could write. What's the bad news?'

'I haven't written any for ages.'

'I see,' Richard said. He picked up her drink and handed it to her. 'You look like you need this.' And took a long, thoughtful mouthful of his own.

'Bit of a block,' she said. 'That and a certain handsome man in my life distracting me.'

'Oops, sorry about that.' He frowned. 'Why don't we arrange a little break somewhere? Bring your laptop.'

Emily smiled at him. 'That would be nice.' Clinking glasses with him.

'Who knows. I may give you inspiration.'

Emily leant across and kissed him on the lips. 'I'm sure you will.'

I slumped onto the settee back at my flat. Richard having dropped me off home after our meal. Inspired by Oliver's phone call, and the promise of the advance, I managed to do some writing. It's marvellous how someone dangling a financial carrot under your nose galvanises you. I'm delighted with the way the story's taking shape. I decided to make Grace, one of the characters, a creative writing teacher. Not unlike myself. What's that maxim? Write what you know. My most productive day for some time. Maybe the timescale the publishers have given me isn't so daunting after all. I'm hoping Richard can help spur me on, rather than slow me down. I've fallen for him massively. I hardly think of Paul these days, and when I do, the hurt and regret aren't there anymore. I've definitely moved on. One of the male characters in my book, Ricky, I've loosely based on Richard. Although I would never admit this to him.

CHAPTER FIVE

JUNE 2013 – Ricky read the paper while he waited for Grace. She finally descended the stairs and entered the lounge. 'I hope I have everything.' Flopping into the chair opposite him she took a deep breath.

'What about your laptop?' Glancing over the top of his newspaper he pulled his glasses down to the bridge of his nose.

'Here,' she said, tapping on the side of her bag.

'And the lesson plans you spent half the night doing?'

'Yeah. Got those too.'

Ricky nodded. 'Good.'

Grace stood, holding out her arms. 'Are you ready then?'

'Me? I've been ready for ages.'

'Well, let's get going. I don't want to be late on my first day.'

Grace sat next to Ricky and rummaged inside her bag.

He placed his hand on hers. 'Grace, you'll be fine. Stop worrying.'

'I can't help it. I want everything to go well.'

'I know you do, but you'll be great. Where's the uber-confident woman I love?'

'Love?'

He smiled. 'Did I say love? I meant like.'

'You can't take it back. Once you've said it.'

'I won't then. Love it is.'

Grace smiled, tapping Ricky's hand as he changed gear. 'Good. Love sounds better.'

Ricky glanced across at her. 'Well?'

'Well what?'

'Aren't you going to reciprocate?'

Grace laughed. 'That's not how it works. You don't tell someone you love them so you can get one back.'

'But now I feel as if I've given up a part of myself and it's unrequited.'

'That's life. One of us had to crack first, and it appears it was you.'

Ricky comically frowned. 'But you do love me?'

Grace smiled. 'Like. I like you.'

He pouted back at her. 'Where do you want dropping off?'

'Southfield Road. Near the junction with Woodlands Road.'

'Yes, ma'am.'

She nudged him. 'What did you tell work?'

He raised his eyebrows. 'I told them I had a dental appointment. A problem with a premolar.'

Grace put a hand on her chest. 'Oh, Ricky. You lied for me?'

'That's the type of thing you do when you *love* someone.' Placing his left hand on his heart, he blew her kiss.

'I could have got a taxi.'

'Yes. You could have.' He pulled the car up on the side of the road. 'But you'd have missed out on all this terrific conversation.'

She opened the car door and clambered out. 'True. See you tonight?' Leaning across, she planted a kiss on his lips.

'About seven?'

'Yeah. Seven's good.'

'Hope everything goes well. Break a leg,' Ricky said

Grace stopped, crossed her fingers and closed the door. 'So do I,' she said through the glass. She waited for him to spin the vehicle around, and as he passed her she waved, mouthing, *I love you*.

Grace grabbed a coffee and mounted the stairs to her classroom. Taking off her coat, she removed her laptop and paperwork from her bag. Positioning herself at the head of the u-shaped ring of chairs, she waited.

The door opened, and Janet – her course co-ordinator – walked in, carrying a small book. She smiled at Grace and ambled closer. 'Ready, Grace?'

'I think so. I'm a little nervous.'

'We all are the first time. What you need to remember is, the students will be as well. You'll be okay. Just be yourself and follow the plan until you're more confident.'

'I will.'

Janet looked in her diary. 'There's an extra student. Sarah Stainton. You sometimes get people who come along on the day too.''

Grace nodded. 'Sarah Stainton.' Jotting down her name, she paused before resuming.

Janet counted the names in her book. 'That makes ten.'

Grace still deep in thought, glanced at her. 'Yes, ten.'

'Ten's a good start. Easier to manage. What are you doing for lunch?'

Grace shrugged. 'Nothing really. I didn't bring anything. I thought maybe I'd walk into town.'

'Why don't we meet after the lesson and I'll treat you to something.' Edging towards the door, she glanced towards Grace. 'Looks like one of yours now.' A woman appeared outside, her form visible through the glass.

'Right,' Grace said. 'Let's grasp the nettle.'

Sarah was running late. Ben's van choosing this morning of all mornings to decide not to start. After finally coaxing it into life, the pair raced across to Middlesbrough centre. Ben dropped her on Linthorpe Road before setting off for Baker Street to open the shop. Luckily, he didn't have much work on for the next couple of weeks, by which time, Sarah hoped to have employed someone to help out. She galloped up the stairs and located the classroom, paused outside catching her breath. She peered through the thin glass panel in the door at the people seated around the table. Taking a deep breath, she knocked.

Grace stopped talking and turned as Sarah entered. 'Sarah Stainton?' Grace said.

'Yes,' she said. And took a step over the threshold. 'I'm sorry I'm late. Car trouble.'

Grace pointed at one of the vacant chairs. 'Don't worry about that. Grab a seat. You haven't missed much. We were doing our introductions. I'm Grace.' She gestured towards a woman to her right. 'This is Claire, and this is Alan. He was just telling us about himself.'

Sarah positioned herself to Graces left, glancing about at the people around the table. There were nine others, not counting Grace. She listened as each individual took it in turn to introduce themselves. Most seemed, similar to her, beginners. A couple of them, a man and a woman, had attended a creative writing course previously. Finally, Grace looked in her direction.

'Hi everyone,' she began. Forcing a smile at Grace and the others. 'My name's Sarah Stainton. I'm thirty-two. I'm new to writing. I've always loved the written word and thought joining a writing class like this would be a great way of learning the art.'

'Your face seems familiar,' Grace said. 'Where do you work?'

'I run a bookshop in Middlesbrough.'

'Of course. Baker Street.' Sarah nodded. 'I've been in there. It's a lovely shop.' She glanced around at the other people. 'Sarah's shop sells second-hand books as well as new. Isn't that right, Sarah?'

Sarah smiled. 'We do.'

Grace picked up her glasses and popped them on. 'So much better than the bigger shops, like Smiths or Waterstones.' The other people nodded in agreement. 'How's your venture doing?'

She smiled again. 'Very well. I don't think I'll ever get rich by it, but it makes a small profit.'

'Well,' Grace said. 'You'll have to write a best-seller then.' She removed her glasses and dangled them by one of the arms. 'What are you hoping to achieve in this class?'

'I'm not sure. I quite like poetry.'

'I don't think we have a poet in here.' Studying the class. The other people nodded in agreement.

'I'm not very good. I just dabble really.'

'That's fine. There's no pressure. You do what you want to, and I'm sure you'll find your voice. Well ...' Grace put her spectacles back on and clasped her hands together. 'The only way to get better at anything is to practise. So, with that in mind, I'd like you to do a little exercise. Don't worry about how good it is. We all have to start somewhere.'

'Will we have to read out?' asked a lady to her right.

Grace smiled, looking around the class. 'I know it seems daunting, but you will get used to it. However, if anyone doesn't feel comfortable doing so they don't have to.'

Sarah, perched on her seat in the canteen, cradled her cup of coffee. She'd enjoyed her first class. The people seemed friendly, coming from a diverse background. She felt excited too. Grace had given them an assignment to do, and she was eager to get started. She was busy jotting down lines in her notebook when Grace joined her.

'Hi, Sarah.' Grace stood holding a cup.

'Hello,' she replied.

'Writing already?'

'I'm just trying to jot some ideas down.' Closing her notebook, she fixed her attention on Grace.

'You don't mind if I join you, do you?'

'No. Not at all.'

Grace sat opposite. 'I'm waiting for Janet, the course administrator, to arrive. She's taking me out to lunch.'

'Lucky you,' Sarah said. 'Have you been a creative-writing teacher long?'

'No. Not long. I was a primary school teacher for a few years. Then I worked in publishing and now this.'

'Do you write yourself?'

'I dabble. A few short stories and poems. I keep kidding myself I'll write a best-seller one day. What about you? What's your history?'

'Well you know I run a bookshop with Ben, my husband. Ben's a carpenter really. He helps me out when he can.'

Grace smiled. 'No problem with shelves then?'

Sarah smiled back. 'No.'

'I'm trying to place your accent?'

'Reading. Well … just outside there, should I say.'

Grace nodded. 'I had a friend who moved to Reading.'

'I moved away in my teens. Lived in London for a while and ended up here after I met someone from Teesside.'

'Ben?'

Sarah squirmed in her seat. She hadn't given Aaron a thought for months, managing to keep those memories buried. 'No. I met someone called … Aaron …' His name stumbling from her lips. Tears formed in her eyes and Sarah put a shaky hand to her mouth. 'I'm sorry,' she said.

Grace leant in closer, putting a hand on Sarah's arm. 'It's all right. Don't worry about it.' Grace opened her handbag and handed her a tissue.

'Thanks,' she said. Dabbing her eyes with the tissue.

'Emotion's good,' Grace said, 'If you're going to write effectively, you need to get in tune with your emotions.'

Sarah turned away as another woman arrived.

Grace pointed at Sarah. 'Janet. This is one of my students.'

Sarah composed herself. 'Hi.' Offering her hand.

Janet shook it warmly. 'How did you enjoy the first lesson?'

Sarah glanced at Grace and smiled. 'Very much.'

'Good, good,' Janet said. 'I'm afraid I'll have to drag Grace away from you. I'm buying her lunch. On expenses, of course … You could join us if you like?'

'That's kind of you,' Sarah said. 'But I'm meeting my husband.'

Grace and Sarah stood. Janet held up a finger as her mobile sounded, turning away from the other two women to answer it.

Grace placed a hand on Sarah's arm again. 'You ok?'

'Yes, thanks.'

Grace hugged Sarah, smiled and turned following the waving Janet. Sarah sat again, admonishing herself for allowing her emotions to get the better of her. Her phone sounded.

'Hi, gorgeous,' Ben said. 'How did it go?'

'Really well.'

'The shop's rammed. I'm going to struggle to get away. I don't suppose—'

'I'll grab a sandwich or something,' she said. 'I'll be ten to fifteen minutes.'

'Ok,' Ben said. 'Love you.'

'Love you.' She hung up and stared at the phone. 'More than I could say,' Sarah whispered to herself.

CHAPTER SIX

OCTOBER 2014 - Emily lay on the lounger beneath the hot, Ibizan sunshine, opening her eyes as the sun was momentarily blocked by someone. Richard stood next to her holding two drinks.

Emily stared up, shielding her eyes from the blinding sunlight. 'Where have you been, fella?'

He held out one of the drinks to her. 'Places.'

'It's a little early for these isn't it?' Glancing at her watch, she accepted the drink from him.

Richard lowered himself onto the sunbed next to hers. 'Nonsense my dear. It's ten at night somewhere in the world.'

Emily took a swig. 'Well all right. But I want it noted I'm doing this under sufferance.'

Richard leant forward and kissed her on the lips. 'Thanks.' He smiled. 'The sacrifices you're prepared to make for me are ...' He put his free hand up to his eyes, and pretended to cry. 'Just incredible. I don't know what to say.'

'Yeah, yeah, whatever,' Emily said. 'You still haven't told me where you've been?'

Richard placed his drink down on the floor, and plonked himself onto the seat next to Grace. 'Remember what the Rep told us on the way here?'

Grace looked skywards and rolled her eyes. 'Not really. I tend to zone out when they start rabbiting on. They're usually trying to squeeze money out of you.'

'Apparently, Ibiza has the most amazing sunsets and I thought—'

Emily sat upright and turned square to him, placing her hands on her heart. 'And you've got me one?'

Smiling, he theatrically swivelled his face away. 'If you're not going to take this seriously—'

Emily put a hand on his cheek and turned his face so they were looking directly at each other. She playfully pouted. 'I'm sorry. Please go on.'

He turned away again. 'I can't now. The moments passed. Here's me trying to be romantic and—'

'You weren't very romantic this morning in our apartment when I wanted to …'

He swung around to face her again. 'You're nothing but a wanton hussy, Emily. We had sex twice. We can't spend all day in bed. You're supposed to be writing.'

Emily edged her face closer. 'I have been. While you were out galivanting. Managed quite a bit, actually.'

'Really? What did you write?'

'The female character, Grace, I've decided, runs a creative writing course.'

'Like you.'

Emily smiled. 'Like me. That's where she meets Sarah.'

'The woman who runs the bookshop?'

'You've got a good memory,' she said.

'For some things.'

'So, big boy. We could spend a little more time in bed. I need a sex-scene for my book. You could help me out.'

Richard stifled a smile. 'Anyway, as I was saying. The sunsets here are fantastic. I thought we could watch it tonight.'

'There will definitely be one then?'

Richard moved his face closer, their lips all but touching. 'Oh yeah. It's the law. I've booked us a table at Café Mambo. The best place to view it from.'

Emily placed a featherlike touch of her lips on his. 'How about we go up to our apartment and get ready. I want to look my best for this sunset.'

'The sunset's hours away.'

She put her hand on Richard's thigh allowing her fingers to slip inside the bottom of his shorts. 'We'll have to find something to kill time then.'

'What did you have in mind?'

She moved her mouth around to his ear. 'We'll just extemporise.'

'Good word. There's something incredibly sexy about an intelligent woman. Can we finish these drinks first?'

'Of course. I can do patience.'

He glanced down at the front of his shorts and raised his eyebrows. 'I can't go anywhere at the moment. These shorts don't leave a lot to the imagination.'

She laughed, adopting a mock, shock-horror face. 'My God! It's huge.'

Reclining back on his sunbed, he pulled a nearby towel across his waist. 'Give me a couple of minutes, and I'll be right there.'

Emily eyed the bulge. 'Isn't it a shame to waste it?'

'They're like buses, Emily.'

Picking up her drink, she stood. 'Don't be long.' She winked at him, sashayed her way around the pool, and hurried into the hotel.

Emily lay in bed almost asleep as Richard slipped beneath the covers and caressed her. She sighed as his soft hand travelled the length of her body, from her shoulder down to her thigh. She eased onto her back, Richard softly nuzzling her ear. His mouth pressed to hers, gently at first but then with more urgency. He moved to her neck, delicately kissing the front of it. Emily allowed her head to fall back submissively, delighting in the moment. She pulled him closer, the two of them moving in synergy. Their passion continued its ascent, her body suffused with energy and subsumed with desire. She drew him nearer still. Her skin tingled at his touch as invisible sparks ricocheted from her. The pleasure slowly approaching ecstasy, flirting briefly with the outskirts of pain. She closed her eyes, dismissing the least beneficial of her senses. Her pleasure reached an apogee and sustained it for what seemed like an eternity before embarking on its slow descent. Her body quivered and throbbed with rapturous satisfaction, and as she opened her eyes, she felt Richard slow, his breath held for a second or two before he let out a moan. He dropped his head onto her shoulder and kissed her neck again. Emily gasped as the pair finally slowed to nothingness. He eased onto his side, gently cupping her chin, and kissed her. Emily ran her fingers across his chest. He gazed at her, love reflected in his smile. She smiled back and stretched up to kiss him.

'I love you,' he whispered.

'I love you too,' she said.

Placing her head on his chest as he stroked her hair. Richard closed his eyes as post-coital tiredness overwhelmed him. Emily closed hers as well. The soporific effects of the alcohol and her exertions, coupled with the metronomic beating of his heart, gently delivering her into the arms of Morpheus.

I lay back in bed as Richard showered, and smiled to myself. There's something wonderful about making love with someone you genuinely want to spend time with. Sex, as a physical act, while enjoyable, sometimes extremely enjoyable, lacks something. It sounds silly, and I would never say this to anyone, not even Lisa, but it's much more than the physical act. I don't know how Richard feels, men tend to be more guarded. Perhaps in time, he will open up. Or maybe he won't. I think I'm falling for him deeply. When I'm in his arms, it feels so special. My clumsy words cannot do justice to how I feel. I would stretch for a metaphor, but again, this would not do it justice. Is what I'm experiencing only infatuation, or something more profound? It is possibly the doubts I possess which keep me tethered and stop me from falling totally. Should I cut the ropes? Should I shut my eyes and tumble headlong into him?

Richard held onto Emily's hand as they sauntered from the hotel and turned onto the beach. Bending down she removed her sandals, allowing them to hang loosely in her free hand. She gently tugged him back. 'Aren't we getting a taxi?'

'Of a sort.' Nodding towards the furthest end of the beach. 'A water-taxi. It's only fifteen minutes to San Antonio Bay.'

'Water taxi? How civilised.'

They stopped outside a bar, and Richard viewed the chalkboard menu. 'We've just got time to have a quick one before the next taxi arrives.'

Emily pulled him close. 'Here. In broad daylight. Won't we be arrested?'

He gave her a peck on the cheek. 'No, my dear. Drinking is legal in Ibiza.'

She gave a wide-eyed look at him. 'Drink. I thought you meant ...'

He smiled. 'Sex on the beach?' Pointing at the drinks menu.

'Will I get an umbrella?'

'If you behave yourself you will.' He patted her bottom as she mounted the steps.

Richard and Emily reclined at the rear of the boat as it stitched its way across the fabric of the water. The cool breeze blowing Emily's hair into a majestic mane behind her. The sun shimmering in the sky. She pulled her mobile from her handbag and pointed it at the pair of them. 'Smile. This is gorgeous.' Tossing back her hair.

'It is. Wait until you see the sunset.'

'How do you know? Have you seen one before?'

'I've seen pictures. On postcards in the shop over the road from the hotel.'

Emily scoffed. 'Pictures? I hope the real thing's a good deal better than a picture. You've given it such a wonderful build up. I don't like anti-climaxes.'

Richard smiled. 'It will be. Another one or two of those cocktails and we'll find anything amazing.'

'God yeah. How much vodka was in mine? I'm feeling a bit tipsy.'

He put his arm around her, pulling her into his body. 'Plenty more to come as well.'

'How far is the restaurant when we get off?'

He reached into his back pocket and plucked a piece of paper from it. 'I'm not sure, but I have a map. It doesn't look far though.'

Emily snatched it from Richard's grasp and viewed it. 'Maps are sneaky. Things don't appear far on them, but in reality, they're miles apart. Something to do with the scale, I believe.' She smiled at him and winked.

He grabbed it from her. 'Leave the map reading to me. It's a well-known fact, women don't understand them.'

Emily playfully punched him. 'That's so sexist.'

He raised his eyebrows. 'It's true. Something to do with evolution.'

'No it's not. That's a myth. Give me the map, and I'll prove you wrong.'

He shook his head. 'No way. We'll miss the sunset.'

Emily held out a hand. 'The sun's in the sky. How the hell can we miss it? The map … Please.'

He pushed his face nearer to hers. 'A kiss and I will.'

Emily snapped her head away. 'That's blackmail. I don't respond to blackmail.'

He held out the map, waving it next to her face. 'It's negotiation, not blackmail. That's the price.'

She grappled for the map, her and Richard wrestling over it. They ceased the battling and Richard seizing an opportunity, kissed her. 'That wasn't so hard, was it?' Richard said.

The pair viewed the other occupants of the boat, all of which were watching them. Emily, with her finger and thumb, took the map from his hand and the duo composed themselves.

She studied it. 'Now. Which way up does it go again?'

Richard smiled and nudged her gently, nodding towards the approaching dock. 'Let's see how good you are then.'

The waiter showed them through the mass of other diners to their table. They sat, and the waiter handed them each a menu.

Richard picked his up, and began to peruse it. 'Just in time.' Nodding towards the sky.

'I told you I could read maps.'

Richard glanced across at Emily. 'Mmm … Wine?'

Emily nodded enthusiastically at him. 'White please.'

'A bottle of Pinot Grigio?' Richard asked.

She looked up from her menu and at the waiter. 'Pinot Grigio please.' The waiter thanked them and left.

Richard studied his menu. 'See anything you fancy? Apart from me.'

She planted her elbows on the table and placed her face between her hands. 'You'd be way too fattening. The carbonara I think.'

'You always order carbonara.'

'I like it. It's my favourite dish. Why change a winning formula?'

'Why indeed. I'll have the seafood risotto.'

She surveyed the scene outside at the mass of people congregating on the beach below. 'There must be hundreds.'

Richard followed Emily's gaze. 'There's a show after the sun goes down.'

Emily comically raised her eyebrows. 'I bet you say that to all the girls?'

He edged closer to her. 'Only one.'

She turned and faced him, taking hold of his hands. 'I love this holiday. I've never been happier. I really mean that.'

He brushed a stray piece of hair from her face. 'Me too.'

They ate as the sun descended towards the sea. The calypso, orange disc, shimmering slowly and majestically melted away. As if the sea itself was extinguishing the massive ball of fire.

Richard took a sip of wine. 'Of course, it's just an illusion.'

Emily cocked her head. 'What is?'

'The sun. As we're watching it cross the horizon, the sun has already vanished. It's only a reflection you're seeing.'

She frowned. 'You're making it up.'

'I'm not. I saw it on Q.I.'

'Honestly?' she said.

'Cross my heart. Stephen Fry wouldn't lie, would he?'

Emily leant in close to him. 'I don't suppose he would.' Clasping hold of his hand, she gazed deeply into his eyes. 'Thanks for this.'

'Did you enjoy the sunset?'

'It was wonderful. Almost spiritual.'

He reached into his pocket and pulled something out, placing the small box on the table in front of her. He smiled and leant back in his chair. Emily stared at the box and then at Richard. Picking it up she gazed into his eyes again. 'This isn't what I think it is, is it?' she said.

His smile fell away. He dropped his head slightly. 'I've never felt like this about anyone, Emily. I know it's only been a few months—'

She smiled at him. 'Two and a half, actually.'

He looked away from her and dropped his eyes. 'I've fallen hook, line and sinker for you. I'd love to turn those two and a half months into decades. If you'd let me?'

She opened the box and pulled out the ring, placing the box on the table. 'It's beautiful.' Her eyes now glistening. 'I can't think of anyone else I'd like to spend the rest of my life with.'

Richard turned and met her gaze. He took the ring from her hand and slowly slid it onto her finger. 'I love you … So much.'

'I love you too.' She reached across the table to kiss him as applause from nearby people rang out.

I crept from our bed as Richard slept, collected my laptop and positioned myself at the table on the terrace. What a fantastic day yesterday was. Richard's proposal came completely out of the blue. At no time have I felt happier. It inspired me. My mind flooded with ideas for my book, making sleep impossible. My word count on this holiday has sky-rocketed. Quite possibly, almost certainly, for the first time in my life, I'm truly in love.

CHAPTER SEVEN

ONE WEEK LATER – Emily stood in front of the mirror and pulled the dress up pushing her arms through the straps. Richard appeared and put his arms around her, gently kissing her neck.

She closed her eyes and tilted her head back. 'Mmm.'

'Do you want a hand with your dress?' he whispered.

'Only if you're fastening it up. We haven't time for any funny business.'

'You normally make time.' Allowing his right hand to slide to the front of her dress and slowly descend, stopping at the line of her panties.

Emily groaned. 'We can't. It's not fair. The taxi will be here soon. If I give in to you, I'll need another shower.'

He playfully nibbled her ear, his erection pressing against Emily's buttocks. 'You're right.' Stepping back, he pulled the zip on Emily's dress to the top.

She turned, leaning back with her hands on the dressing table, her eyes wide and her face a frown. 'You're a fine one. Getting a girl all worked up and leaving her high, and not so dry.'

Richard smiled, turned away and ambled towards the door. Stopping at the threshold, he spun around. 'I'll see you downstairs.' He winked.

Emily smiled and turned to face the mirror. 'Tease,' she murmured to herself.

Richard helped Emily from the taxi. She linked his arm, and carrying a plastic bag in her other hand, she and Richard entered the restaurant. A waiter led the couple through the diners to a table at the furthermost end of the room. Lisa and Tim stood as they neared. The four exchanging hugs and kisses before sitting.

Lisa fixed Emily with a stare. 'Dinner?' she said. A smile appearing on her face. 'Must be important?'

Emily glanced in Richard's direction and held out her hand. Lisa took hold of it and studied the ring. 'Wow. Clearly sunbathing wasn't the only thing you got up to on holiday.'

Tim patted Richard on the arm. 'Congratulations you two.' Leaning forward to plant a peck on Emily's cheek.

Emily smiled, nudging Richard. 'This fool has gone and proposed to me. I'm not even pregnant or anything.'

Richard clasped hold of her hand and gazed into her eyes. 'Yeah. Moment of weakness, Tim. She got me drunk on Sangria.'

Tim nodded. 'Ah. The old, *get you drunk so you'll propose, plan.*'

Richard chuckled. 'Yeah. And of course, once you've proposed, there's no reneging.'

Tim laughed. 'This one.' Nodding at Lisa. 'Used a similar ploy on me. Look at me now? A shadow of the man I was.'

'Have you fixed a date yet?' Lisa asked.

'Give us a break,' Emily said. 'We've only just got back.'

Lisa beamed. 'I'll need a hat.'

Emily squeezed Richard's hand. 'We're not planning a huge white wedding or anything. Just a modest affair.'

Richard glanced at Emily and turned to Lisa and Tim. 'I've told her she can have whatever she wants.'

Emily patted Richard on the arm. 'A simple service is all I want.'

Lisa shuffled closer to Emily, glancing over towards Tim and Richard, the two men buried in conversation at the bar. 'Well. This is a turn up for the books.'

Emily took a sip from her glass and placed it down. 'Why? You told me Richard and I make a perfect couple.'

'I did. I still do. I knew you and Richard were getting on well. But marriage?'

'I never expected him to propose. It came as a complete shock. He took me to a lovely restaurant in Ibiza and asked me to marry him as the sun set in the sky.'

Lisa placed a hand on Emily's. 'I'm so happy for you.'

Emily glanced towards Richard at the bar and then fixed Lisa with a stare. 'He's the real deal. I've never felt like this about anyone. I'm ...'

Lisa gently squeezed her friend's hand. 'In love?'

Emily bit her lip. 'Yes. I suppose I am. I have this feeling ...'

Lisa frowned. 'What feeling?'

'I can't explain. Just an odd feeling something's going to happen to spoil all of this.'

Lisa gently shook Emily's hand. 'You're being silly.'

'I want this to work so much,' Emily said. 'I've never had much luck with men, and then Richard came into my life. I can't shake the feeling

I don't deserve to be happy. That something is going to come along and spoil all this.'

Lisa leant back in her chair as Richard and Tim returned with their drinks. Richard handed Emily a glass of wine. 'What are you two plotting?'

'Nothing,' Emily said. 'Girls talk that's all.'

Lisa smiled at Richard. 'Emily was telling me you proposed under a setting sun. How romantic.'

Richard took hold of Emily's hand and kissed the back of it. 'Alcohol, sun, sea and sand. And the most gorgeous woman I've ever met. How could I not?'

NOVEMBER 2014 – Emily entered the care home. Waving at a few of the staff as she walked through it. Making her way along the corridor, she stopped at the threshold of a door and looked over at an old man seated in a high-backed chair staring at the television. Emily forced a smile and walked over to the TV, switching it off. The old man remained motionless. Oblivious to this or Emily. She sat next to him and clasped hold of his hand.

'Hi, Dad. How are you?'

The old man lifted his head slightly and turned to face her. 'Is that you, Mary?'

'No. Mam's not here. She's …' Emily paused and put a hand on his cheek.

'Our Tom was here earlier,' her dad said.

She lowered her eyes. 'Are you sure? Australia's a long way to come for a visit.'

'He's bought himself a new bike. A *BSA A65 star*. He said he'll let me have a go at the weekend.'

'You mean Uncle Tom. I thought you meant …' She smiled and shook her head.

'Will Patch need feeding?'

'Not yet, Dad.' She patted his arm.

'He's a bugger when he wants feeding.'

Emily put a hand on his cheek, again. 'Who am I, Dad?'

The old man furrowed his brow and stared at Emily. His face etched in concentration.

'I'm Emily, Dad.'

'Emily?'

'Your daughter. Your little girl.' Her eyes glistened.

The old man screwed up his face, slowly shaking his head. 'I don't know … Emily …' Putting his hand up to his eyes he rubbed them.

She gently squeezed his hand. 'Don't worry about it. Do you want your music on?'

He smiled and nodded. 'Sinatra.'

'I knew you'd say that.' Placing a hand on his face, the old man smiled back at her.

She stood and wandered across to the CD player, switching it on. The music filled the room with sound. The old man leant back in his chair and drummed the arm with his right hand.

Emily picked up a brush and started to tidy his hair. 'I'm getting married. His name's Richard. He proposed to me on holiday. Needs his head examining if you ask me.'

The old man indifferent to her, continued to tap his fingers. She returned to her seat as the CD continued to play, holding on tight to his hand. Occasionally he'd glance at her and smile. The final song finished and standing again, she turned off the player.

She picked up a photo album and opened it, placing it on her father's lap. 'Shall we look at some old snaps?'

The old man smiled, slowly running his fingers across the pictures. He stopped at one of a small girl wearing a pink dress. 'Our Emily,' he said. 'We bought her that dress for her tenth birthday. We had a party in the house. Her mam put on a lovely spread.'

'Can you remember who was at the party?'

He turned and gazed at her. 'Our Tom.' The old man chuckled. 'He made himself sick eating too much.'

She flicked over the page. 'Who's this?' Pointing at a photo of a boy and girl together.

'That's our Emily and Tom. They'd fight like cat and dog those two. Trying to get them in the same photo was a job in itself.' He giggled. 'They loved each other though.' His face took on a serious look. 'When they got older. Always covering up for each other. I knew though. They must have thought I was daft.' Tapping the side of his nose, he chuckled.

'Where's Tom now?'

'Tom ... I don't know.' The old man frowned. 'He'll be at school. He'd better be.' And laughed again.

Emily put her hand on her dad's cheek. 'Where have they gone, Dad?' she whispered. 'Those precious memories. All those years?'

The old man turned the page and tapped at a photo. 'That's Anthony Watson from around the corner. Cheeky little bugger he is. I've told our Tom to stop knocking about with him. He'll get him into serious bother.'

Emily smiled. 'He's a doctor now.' Patting her father's hand, she shook her head.

The old man reclined in his chair and closed his eyes. 'Aye. A right little bugger.'

She stood, bending lower to kiss him on the cheek. 'I love you, Dad.' Her eyes glistening with tears.

He opened his eyes and smiled at her. Lifting a hand, he placed it on her cheek. 'Emily. My angel.'

She hugged him and put the TV back on. The old man's eyelids briefly laboured with gravity before slowly falling down. She turned, stopped at the door for one final glance, and left.

Emily sat in her car and searching her contacts, phoned.

'Hello,' said a voice, bathed in tiredness.

She glanced at her watch. 'I haven't woken you, have I?'

'Sis?' he said. 'I was about to get up.'

'I visited Dad today.'

'How is he?' said her brother.

'About the same.'

'We're thinking of coming over later this year. I've been doing a bit extra at work to save up for the flights.'

'That's great. I have some news of my own.'

'Oh yeah. Good, I hope?'

'It is,' Emily said.

EMILY'S DIARY

NOVEMBER 15th 2014 - *Visited Dad today. His dementia is worsening I think. I often find myself asking: Where do the memories go? Those wonderful bits of information that link us to our past. Do they fall through the cracks in the pavement of life, never to be seen again? It's sad to think that the most precious of gifts we ever possess are so easily lost.*

Phoned Tom and lied to him about Dad. I couldn't bear to tell him the truth. What can he do when he's in Australia? I felt the need to speak with him though. Sometimes in life, you need to talk to someone familiar. Someone who was there with you in your past. Someone you fought and cried with, someone you loved and laughed with. Someone who felt the razor-sharp-sting of loss with you. I thought hearing his voice would be a comfort to me. But, when you need somebody and they're miles away, it brings it home to you. To paraphrase Leo Sayer: A telephone can never take the place of someone's smile.

NOVEMBER 16th 2014 – *Went and put flowers on Mum's grave. Why do we do this? Make a pilgrimage to the place where you buried a loved one. I'm an atheist and Mum's long gone. I need photographs now to remind me of what she looked like, and I haven't viewed any in years. Looking at them fills me with* *deep sorrow. Yet part of me feels guilty for not. When she died, I secretly wished it had been Dad. A horrible thought to harbour because I love my dad. It was as if my childish thoughts could only reach a satisfactory accord if I chose between them. Daughters need their mum's, they're so very special. In dying – when I was still young – Mum and I were robbed of so much. Deprived of all those fantastic memories, destined never to be written. In the book of life, there are many blank pages.*

Blank Pages

A cerulean landscape shone, the presage to my dawn
The blinding glow of maternal gaze, to which I would be drawn
And souls that would forever beat, in symmetry and time
With heartfelt joy and shared belief, our love began its climb
But then as fate walked forward now, and tugged so tightly at my strings
You stepped from light into the dark, as life unfurled its earthly wings
Your illness crept with stealth and guile and stole away those priceless days
And features that had once burned bright, now hide behind a temporal haze
I long to feel that missing touch, I long to view that wonderous smile
I ache for what was never ours, marooned within my lonely isle
Our memories quill laid down in prime, the ink of life was left to dry
Now only pictures fill my void, and only blackness colours my sky
A paltry link to what I lost, a mother's love, endlessly clings
The pages of life eternally blank, a sentence which forever stings

CHAPTER EIGHT

The Final Journey

A pall drifts steadily across a sullen sky as sunshine bows and takes its leave.
And Gold and yellow teardrops tumble dolefully from stark and naked trees.
Divested and denuded branches look on, and bend their heads in reverence.
While shuffling, mournful pilgrims follow suit in sombre melancholy deference
Sadness falls across a waiting throng, infecting sorrow strips happiness from all around.
As eyes turn left and meet the black and stately ship, which glides towards its final resting ground.
Enormity of loss in splendid oak, through solemn glass, bedecked in floral solitude.
Draws painfully to passage end, a citadel where many mass, a fortress of the blackest mood.
And memories lofted high on mighty shoulders of the few; march forward on
Sheep-like kin and friends before, are sucked through doors towards the gone.
As death walks tall amongst the living and follows us all from birth to wake
Realisation dawns across assembled crowd, a journey which we all must make.

FEBRUARY 2015 - Grace made her way through the gates of the crematorium and following the signs to the car park, pulled up at the first available space. Turning the engine off, she leant back in the seat and blew out hard. The effort of getting herself ready for the funeral and driving to it, sapping her resolve. She wanted to leave. Start the engine and head off home. She wouldn't be missed. Nobody would even know who she was. But she needed to come. She had reasoned, and counter-reasoned. Her sense of doing the right thing gnawed at her relentlessly. Grace sighed. A tired, resigned, acceptance of a sigh. Reluctantly she stepped out of the car. The chill breeze eliciting a gasp from her. Pulling the collar of her overcoat around her neck, she trudged across the gravel car park with leaden feet, and made her way towards the large group of mourners assembled outside the chapel. People chatted and shook hands with friends and family. Some hugged each other. A tangible sign of their grief. As she surveyed the scene of emotional carnage *she had caused,* Grace lowered her head. The heavy weight of guilt resting uncomfortably on her shoulders. She lifted up her head once more as the throng gazed along the road. Looking to her right, an audible gasp escaped her mouth as the black vehicles made their way towards them. People jostled in readiness as the first vehicle – the one carrying the coffin – drew to a halt outside the doors to the chapel. Sarah's name emblazoned in white carnations along the side of the casket. Grace backed away a little, moving further from the roadside as the second car pulled up. She reached into her coat pocket for the comfort-blanket handkerchief placed there earlier. Gripping it fiercely in her hand, she turned away as the doors to the second car opened. Not wanting to look, she resisted until she could do so no more. Her head turned, and she stared straight into the face of Ben. Sadness etched deeply into his features. A woman in her late fifties or early sixties – she guessed – linked his arm while another female gently stroked the top of his back. Grace edged further back as the miasma of sadness, his sadness, their grief, swirled around her. She lifted the piece of cloth to her face and shakily dabbed at the tears now forming in her eyes. The coffin hoisted onto the shoulders of six men, with Ben at the front. She watched as the men crept inside the building, sucking the large group of people behind them through the doors. She waited until the last moment and slowly, begrudgingly, followed. The seats by now all occupied and Grace, along with a number of others stood against the back wall. The coffin decorously covered in blooms taking centre stage at the opposite end. A hush descended in the room, and a man took his place behind the lectern.

The ceremony crawled by. Words were said, and hymns were sung. Tears shed and stories told. With each passing second, the guilt within Grace grew. It began as a small knot in the pit of her stomach but had now mushroomed to massive proportions. She closed her eyes and selfishly wished for it to be over.

Grace was first out of the doors, racing across the carpark towards her car, stopping at the car to gather her breath. Her hands resting on the top of the vehicle as her heart thudded in her chest. She felt dizzy. Her head spun as images from the funeral mocked her. She staggered away from the car and vomited. The paltry breakfast she'd managed to force down expelled onto the grass. She wiped her mouth with the handkerchief and turned. Embarrassment filled her as she glanced about. She was alone. Fumbling for her car keys, she opened the door. Struggling to place the keys in the ignition, she eventually managed, the engine roaring into life. Grace backed out and sped off along the route she'd arrived by. Only realising she was travelling along a one-way system the wrong way when she narrowly avoided hitting another car. Onto Acklam Road she screeched, and set off home. The sanctuary the vehicle briefly offered her rapidly diminished as the guilt within her demanded her attention. She fought as images swamped her head. The hearse, the coffin and Ben. His face an image forever branded deeply into the dermis of her mind.

Her journey home, though short, seemed endless to her. Finally, she found herself outside her flat and let herself in throwing her coat onto the hall table. Bounding up the stairs and into the bathroom she dropped onto the floor and retched over the bowl. Her stomach now empty, offering nothing but a sickly taste in her mouth. She slumped against the wall and waited, her nausea gradually receding. Grace clambered to her feet and staggered towards the bedroom. Door frames and furniture assisting her effort to remain upright. Kicking off her shoes she fell onto the bed, pulling the duvet around herself like a defensive shield. The room was dark, the curtains still drawn. Grace pulled her knees up to her chest and gripped them tightly. The images returned. The brief respite her mind had given her while she was sick, now gone. They hectored and taunted her. Her body wrapped up like a punch-drunk boxer against the ropes desperately trying to avoid the blows raining down. They came quickly. Her dam of grief well and truly breached as memories from her past bludgeoned their way into her consciousness, joining forces with the day's events, creating a hurricane of guilt which battered and crashed around her. Grace moved a hand to her stomach, the ghost of her unborn child stirring within. She gripped the duvet and closed her eyes as tight as she could. Unable to avoid the onslaught, she started to cry. The tears mercilessly pushing their way past sealed lids and as Grace lay there, in the quiet of her bedroom, she cried and cried and cried.

The ringing of the doorbell was incessant. Grace blearily opened her eyes. Unsure of what time or even what day it was, she sat up in bed. Turning and planting her feet on the floor. The muscles in her stomach ached, a leftover from her retching. The doorbell sounded again, and then a loud knock. She stood, her balance just about sufficient to keep her upright. She stumbled into the hall, her head a fuzzy ache.

'Grace,' shouted Lucy, through the letterbox. 'Please open the door, Grace.'

Grace brought her hands to her face and rubbed them to push away the clouds clogging her mind. Staggering towards the door, she fumbled at the latch and pulled it open. Turning instantly away from her friend's gaze. Lucy and Tim followed her into the lounge. Grace slumped noisily into an armchair.

Lucy eased into a chair opposite her friend. 'I tried ringing but your phone—'

'I pulled it out.'

'And your mobile?'

'I switched it off. I didn't feel much like talking.'

'Should I make a cup of tea?' Tim asked. Grace glanced in his direction. A false smile briefly appearing on her lips.

'Please.' Lucy smiled at her husband. Tim left, closing the door behind him.

Lucy leant forward. 'I was worried.' A slight quiver diluted her voice. 'I made Tim bring me here … I—'

'I went to the funeral.' A deafening silence descended. Grace shrank away from her friend's stare, towards a meaningless point in space.

Lucy moved nearer still. Perching on the edge of her seat within touching distance. 'It was an accident.' Her words stripped of anything convincing.

Grace sneered. 'A random convergence of events?'

'That's all.' With more conviction this time.

'I caused it, Lucy. I set the wheels in motion. Without me, Sarah …' Her name like a poison on her lips constricted and tightened around her throat, sucking the air from her lungs. Grace gasped as the image of Ben engulfed her. Lucy raced across and hugged her friend.

'How could you know what would happen?' Brushing the bedraggled hair from her friend's face, she pulled her close.

'Someone once told me …' Forcing herself to stare at Lucy. 'Guilt is like a ball living within you. You can never subtract from it. You only ever add to it. It's here.' Placing a hand on her chest. 'It will always be here.'

'You shouldn't have gone.' Her voice quivered. 'What did you expect? Funerals are never happy events.'

'I don't know. I just had to go and see Ben.' She sobbed, her hand moving to her mouth seconds too late to stop a cry from escaping.'

'I want you to come to ours. Tim understands. I've told him everything. We've made a bed up for you in the spare room. I won't leave you here on your own.'

Grace nodded acceptance. Her resolve and self-respect now a crumbling ruin. Her self-loathing a towering edifice.

CHAPTER NINE

DIARY OF SARAH-LOUISE WILLIAMS

January 1st, 2012 - *A new year, a new beginning? Aaron didn't come home last night. This has become a regular event. I let the New Year in by myself. Loneliness doesn't come close to how I felt.*

February 4th, 2012 - *Aaron can't conceal the contempt he feels for me these days. I can't remember when I first realised he hated me. He sees other women. I can smell them on his clothes. He doesn't attempt to disguise the fact. How did I end up in this walled garden, looking at nothing but grey skies?*

March 16th, 2012 - *Our fifth wedding anniversary. Aaron brought me flowers and a platinum necklace. I put it with all the other trinkets he's bought me over the years. We went out for dinner and then had sex. The gentle lovemaking of when we first met, long since gone. Afterwards, I curled into a ball and cried while he showered. He can't even stand the smell of me on him now.*

April 10th 2012 - *Aaron came home from the pub in a foul mood. His latest woman must have rejected his advances because he insisted we had sex. When I refused, he grabbed me by the throat. I nearly passed out.*

April 10th 2012 - *I found a packet of tranquillisers at the bottom of one of the drawers. I thought I'd disposed of them all. I desperately wanted to take a couple. The numbness they promote, so tempting. I resisted the urge and put them back where I found them, until I decide what to do with them.*

April 11th 2012 - *Aaron was contrite about Saturday night. He asked for my forgiveness. What could I do? This is my life. This is who I am now.*

May 1st, 2012 - *Aaron hasn't bothered me since … He obviously has a new woman. I've kept the tablets. Just in case.*

May 28th, 2012 - *Aaron staggered home drunk. I'd locked the bedroom door and placed a chair against the handle. He was irate. He shouted obscenities through the door for twenty minutes. My life's ebbing away, like a stream drying under the blistering heat of the summer sun.*

May 31st, 2012 - *I plucked up the courage and told Aaron I wasn't happy. I don't know how I managed to say the words. He sneered at me and called me an ungrateful bitch. He claimed it was me that made him this way. He smashed my favourite ornament on the kitchen floor. It's not the loss of this which matters, it's how easily he can crush me.*

June 7th, 2012 – *I told Aaron I wanted a divorce. I'm not sure where the words came from, but as I said them his face filled with fury. He grabbed me by the arm and threw me across the living room. He pinned me to the floor and told me he'd never give me a divorce before he … I'm battered and bruised inside and out. I cradled the pills and a half bottle of vodka I'd managed to smuggle into the house. Oblivion seems so welcoming. Death beckons to me, constantly.*

JUNE 2012 – Ben Stainton bounded out of his house. Quickly checking the contents of his van, and satisfied he had the tools he needed, he set off. He was already late and hated this. Punctuality was important to him. Skirting the borderline of the speed limit he raced onto the A19, eventually turning off onto the A689. He slowed as he entered the Wynyard estate, simultaneously driving and programming his sat-nav. Finally reaching his destination, he pulled up outside a huge house and got out, marching up the drive towards the door. It swung open as he arrived at it.

'You're late,' the man said. His faced etched with annoyance.

'Sorry about that. The A19's horrendous.'

He tutted. 'I'm late myself now.' Ben followed as he stomped inside, and reflected for a moment. He considered turning around and getting back into his van, but he needed this job. Work was slow at the moment, and Mr Williams was paying him well, so he bit his lip.

The man strode into the dining room, his eyes scanning around, searching for something. 'Sarah! Where the hell are my car keys?' Marching back into the hall he threw up his hands.

A Women came running into the room clutching car keys. 'I've got them here, Aaron.'

Aaron grabbed them from her. 'Why do you have to move things?' He gestured at Ben. 'This is the joiner.'

Ben forced a smile. 'Carpenter.'

The man stood and stared at him for a second. 'Well, whatever you are, my wife will show you where the job is. I've got a meeting.'

'Fine.' A deep frown appeared on Ben's forehead. He needed the money, and it was this, and this alone, that stopped him from walking back out to his van.

Aaron raced towards the open door. 'Make sure he gets it right, Sarah.' Stomping through it and slamming it shut behind him.

'I'm sorry,' Sarah said.

Ben spun around ready to launch a verbal assault but stopped, his eyes meeting the small, timid-looking creature standing before him. She was pretty though, and when she smiled, his anger evaporated.

She lowered her head. 'He's not always like that. He's a bit stressed at the moment. His work's rather demanding.'

Ben smiled back at her. 'It's ok. We all have bad days, Mrs Williams.'

'Sarah,' she said. 'Can I get you a drink? A cup of tea or coffee?'

'I'd better crack on. Just point me in the right direction.'

Ben slumped onto the edge of his bench and rubbed the back of his neck. The cabinet he was constructing beginning to take shape. He turned around on hearing footsteps behind him. Sarah entered carrying a bottle of beer.

She smiled and held it out to him. 'I thought you might be thirsty.'

'I am, but I'm driving.

'It's alcohol-free.' She continued to hold out the bottle to him. 'I've made some lunch. Nothing special, I'm afraid. Just a piece of fish and salad.

'I've brought sandwiches.' He accepted the drink from her.

Sarah lowered her eyes to the floor. 'Oh, I'm sorry.' Turning away from him. 'I should have asked.'

Ben grinned. 'I suppose I could have them for my tea.'

Sarah viewed him again. A broad grin spread across her face. 'Five minutes,' she said, and carefully pushed the hair which had fallen across her eyes, behind her ear.

'Five minutes.' Ben watched as she turned again and walked off.

Ben sat at the table and Sarah placed a plate of food in front of him.

'Thanks,' he said.

She positioned herself opposite. 'Help yourself to the salad.'

He smiled. 'I'm grateful for this. In truth, I wasn't particularly looking forward to my lunch. The ham has seen better days.'

'Doesn't your wife make your sandwiches for you?'

Ben paused placing some of the salad on his plate. 'I'm widowed.'

'I'm sorry. I didn't—'

'It's ok. It was some time ago. To be honest my friends and family tend to avoid talking about Katherine. They think it'll upset me.'

'How long is it …?'

'Ten years.'

Sarah nodded. 'Hasn't there been anyone else since? I don't mean to be ... it's none of my business.'

Ben laughed. 'No.'

Sarah smiled. 'What are you laughing at?'

'You ask a lot of questions. I don't mind though. We have to talk about something.'

'Sorry.' Lowering her eye's a little, she pushed her food around her plate. 'I don't talk to many people these days ... I ...'

'Why's that?'

She dropped her head. 'Aaron's protective ... over-protective. If I'm honest.'

'What about friends and family?'

'My family live down south ... I haven't seen them for some time.'

'Friends?'

Sarah shuffled in her seat. 'I haven't any really. I did have one, Amy. She lived a couple of doors away, but Aaron disliked her. He had words with her husband about something, and that was that.'

Ben lifted a forkful of food to his mouth. 'But surely it's up to you who you are friends with.'

Sarah sighed. 'It's easier this way. I wouldn't want ... Anything for a quiet life.' Briefly staring down at her food, she lifted her head. 'You're making a good job of Aaron's den.'

'Thanks. It's relatively straight-forward.'

'Have you been a carpenter all your life?'

Ben smiled. 'No. I used to be a schoolboy once.'

'I mean, working life.' Lifting her head again, she grinned at him.

Ben smiled back. 'My dad was a carpenter. I worked with him until he retired.'

'Is your fish ok?'

Ben nodded. 'It's excellent.'

'Would you like another beer?'

'No thanks. It was all right, but I can't see the point of non-alcoholic beer. If I'm honest.'

Sarah coughed. 'Aaron won't allow it in the house. His dad was an alcoholic, you see.'

Ben nodded. 'And you?'

She forced a smile. 'I liked a drink, but since I've been with Aaron I haven't ...'

He took a sip of water. 'I see.'

She lowered her gaze. 'I have fruit juice if you'd prefer.' Nodding towards his glass.

'Waters fine.'

'How long will it take you to finish?'

Ben rubbed the stubble on his chin and pondered. 'Most of the week I would say.'

She gazed at him. His eyes lifted to meet hers. 'Maybe I can cook you something tomorrow. I love cooking.'

He smiled at her and nodded. 'I'd like that.'

She lowered her eyes to the table. 'Can we keep this to ourselves? Aaron can get a bit funny about ...'

'Of course.' He continued to gaze at her and Sarah lifted her head again to meet his stare, smiling broadly.

SARAH'S DIARY

June 10ᵗʰ 2012 – *A Carpenter was working at the house this morning. His name's Ben. We ate lunch together while we talked. I can't remember the last time I spoke to a man other than Aaron. Ben's funny, intelligent and incredibly charming. The sun appeared a little brighter today.*

June 11ᵗʰ, 2012 – *Aaron was in a foul mood when he got home last night. He ranted for ages about work before storming out to the pub. His dinner ended up in the bin. I'm ashamed of the amount of food we waste when I think of people who have so little.*

Ben was here again. I cooked a pasta dish for lunch which he loved. He had me laughing out loud at his funny stories. I was rapt, and almost stretched across the table and touched his hand. The time with him, fleeting. When he left, I felt bereft. Why is this?

June 12ᵗʰ, 2012 – *Ben and I ate lunch together again. He brought a couple of beers with alcohol in them, not the disappointing kind Aaron buys. We laughed and talked about lots of things. The only dark cloud on the horizon is that Ben will soon be finished. Probably by Thursday. Dante said, 'There is no greater sadness than remembering a good time when in absolute misery.' Is this how I'll feel when Ben is gone for good?*

Ben dropped his tool bag near to the front door and began gathering up his other things. Sarah appeared at the threshold of the dining room, and gazed towards Ben, watching him as he continued what he was doing. He finished and turned to face her. A huge smile filling his face. She smiled back, and strolled across to him with a piece of paper in her hand. Stopping three or four feet away from him she held it out. 'I've got the cheque Aaron left for you.'

Ben took hold of it and stared at her face. A few seconds passing before she relinquished her grip.

Ben smiled again. 'Thanks for all the meals. You're a fabulous cook.'

'It was a pleasure.'

He glanced towards the door. 'I should get going.'

Sarah nodded, forcing a smile. 'Have you got everything?'

'I think so. I'm terrible for leaving stuff. I've had a good sweep up, but I know how women have a stricter cleaning regimen than most men. You might want to—'

'I'll hoover when you're ...'

Ben held out his hand. 'I hope your husband likes it.'

Sarah took hold of his massive paw. 'I like it.'

He pushed his hand into his pocket and pulled out a small wooden box. Holding it in his palm, he offered it to Sarah. 'I've got you this. As thanks ... For the meals and the chats. I really appreciated it.'

Sarah accepted it from him, scrutinising the tiny object in her hand. An 'S' delicately engraved on the lid. 'Oh Ben.' Clutching the box tightly to her chest. 'You shouldn't waste your money on me.'

'It wasn't expensive. I made it. I couldn't compete with all this.' Gesturing around the room.

Sarah reached out, allowing her hand to gently stroke Ben's. Something she had denied herself from the moment they'd met. He brought his other hand up to touch her cheek. A bed of straw against her lace. She held onto him. Sarah's warmth reflected in her smile.

'I'd better go.' Releasing his grip on her hand while allowing his other to drift away from her face. He turned and opened the door, stepping through and closing it behind him. He threw the tool bag into the back of the van, slamming it shut. Moving around to the driver's side he opened the door, allowing himself a final glimpse. Sarah now stood at the window. She raised her hand and gave a half-hearted wave. He waved back and got into his van. The door closed with a resounding thud. He took a deep breath, started the engine, and then was gone.

June 13th, 2012 – Ben left for the last time today. He made a wooden box with my initial engraved on the lid. Inside, a silver necklace with a dove on it. A symbol of hope. Heaven wouldn't seem so high, I know, if the times gone by, hadn't been so low.

CHAPTER TEN

Ben dropped his van off at his flat, showered, changed and headed to his local. A few of his friends already there when he arrived. After forcing a couple of drinks down, and not much in the mood for drinking, he called a taxi and left, lying to his mates he had a headache.

The taxi pulled up outside his sister's, and after paying the driver Ben knocked.

The door opened. Toby, his brother-in-law, stood there. 'Ben. How are you?' Smiling he offered his hand.

'Very well.' Ben followed the limping Toby – who was assisted by his crutches – inside. 'How's the leg?' Ben asked.

'Much better. It's been like a life sentence. Can't wait to get back on my bike.'

'Where's Mary?'

'In here.' Hobbling into the kitchen. 'Look who I have?'

A woman turned around. 'Well. If it isn't my little brother,' she said, drawing him into a hug and kissing him.

Ben dramatically rolled his eyes. 'Only by a couple of minutes.'

She nodded towards the oven. 'Are you hungry? I've made cottage pie.'

Toby patted Ben on the back. 'Of course he's hungry. He's always hungry.'

Ben smiled. 'I've eaten. But I'll have a drink.'

'Toby. Get Ben a beer will you?' Mary said.

Ben played football in the garden with his nephews as Mary looked out through the french doors. She opened one of them. 'Boys. You need to get yourselves ready. You're going to be late.'

'Five more minutes, Mam,' shouted the taller of the boys.

'No, now. Uncle Ben needs a rest, too.'

The boys traipsed in carrying a football each and headed upstairs. Ben stepped inside and closed the door. 'Where are they off too?'

Mary rolled her eyes. 'Karate. It's their latest fad. It won't last.'

'What about football? Are they still playing?'

Mary glanced up at the ceiling. 'Saturday morning training. Match on Sunday. They're both away this week, too. Toby will have to take one, and I'll take the other. The vagaries of being parents.' Shaking her head.

Ben slumped onto one of the dining chairs. 'I'm knackered. My old bones aren't up to football with youngsters anymore.'

Mary ambled towards the door. 'Get yourself a drink.' Pointing at the fridge. 'I'll just sort these two out.'

She came back into the dining room five minutes later and slumped into a chair opposite him, letting out a huge sigh. 'I hope you've got one of them for me?' Nodding towards the bottle in front of him.

Ben pulled a beer from beneath the table and held it out towards her. She made a grab for it, but anticipating her effort he pulled it away from her.

Mary scowled comically. 'Ben. We're not ten anymore.'

'Here.' Holding it out again.

Mary inched her hand slowly towards the drink and grasping the neck, pulled hard. Ben held on to the bottle firmly.

'Fine.' Relinquishing her grip. 'I'll get one from the fridge.'

He placed the bottle down and pushed it towards her. 'All yours, Sis.'

She snatched the bottle and pulled it to her, taking a large swig, froth flowing from the top as she plonked it down. 'So, Ben Stainton.' Leaning back in her chair. 'What did you really come around for?'

He sipped his drink. 'Can't a brother visit his sister without there being an ulterior motive?'

'No. I know you too well. It comes with being twins. Spill the beans, Bennie-boy.'

'Now who's acting ten?' Slumping back in his chair, he picked up his drink.

She theatrically folded her arms, and glancing away from Ben raised her nose in the air. 'Have it your way.'

He looked directly at her. 'I've met someone.'

Mary turned to face him holding out her arms. 'Right. And ...'

'That's it.'

'That's it? You've met someone. Does she have a name? This someone.'

'Sarah.' Her name stumbling from his lips.

'Is it serious?'

Ben picked at the label on his bottle. 'We haven't even kissed.'

Mary groaned. 'This is like pulling teeth. Come on. Tell me more.'

72

'That's it. We met. I—'

'Like her?'

'Yeah. I suppose I do.'

She rolled her eyes and held out her hands again. 'So ask her out.' Picking her beer back up she gestured at him with the bottle.

'It's not that simple.'

Mary put down her beer. 'Ben. We all loved Katherine. We all miss her, but she wouldn't have wanted you to be alone. It's been ten years. Ten years is plenty. Isn't it?'

'I know.'

'So what's the problem? Doesn't she fancy you?'

He grinned. 'Fancy? It makes us sound like teenagers.'

'Sorry. Is she attracted—'

'She's married.' Dropping a verbal grenade into the conversation.

Mary leant back in her chair. 'Aah. I see.'

He exhaled. 'You don't really … She's unhappy.'

'Has she told you this?'

'Not in so many words.'

'She may be just flirting.' Mary said. 'Women do flirt.'

Ben took a swig of his beer. 'It wasn't like that. I've been doing work at her house, and we got talking.'

'A customer? Come on Ben. I thought you had more sense than that. Falling for a frustrated housewife.'

Ben put down his beer and stood. 'It's not like that.' Turning away from Mary he stared outside. 'You don't understand.'

She stood and ambled over to him putting her arm around his waist and pulling him playfully. 'So explain?'

He sighed. 'I see how unhappy she is. It's written all over her face. Her sadness is palpable.'

'If she feels the same for you as you feel for her—'

Ben rubbed at the stubble on his chin. 'I'm not sure how I feel. I'm a little …'

Mary narrowed her eyes. 'And her husband?'

'I don't know. I don't like him. I didn't from the moment we met. He appears to dominate her. She's a different person when he's not around. She comes alive.'

Mary looked him the eyes. 'If you're right and she's unhappy, she should leave him.'

He sighed. 'She has nobody. She's alone up here. Her family live down south.'

'What about her friends?'

Ben lowered his eyes and shook his head. 'She hasn't any.'

'Have you thought that she may be looking for a way out? You could be a convenient anybody?'

Ben pulled her arm from around him. 'Of course. I'm not stupid, Mary.'

'Why don't you leave it for the moment. If she's serious about you ...'

Ben looked at his sister. 'I should go. I shouldn't have come.'

'Why? You used to tell me everything.'

He put a hand on Mary's arm. 'I'm sorry. I didn't mean to snap.'

Mary forced a smile. 'We're having a barbeque next Saturday. Will you come? Please.'

He forced a smile back. 'What time?'

'About one.'

'I'll be there. ' Planting a kiss on her cheek, he tapped her arm.

Mary hugged him hard. 'I love you, Ben Stainton. If anyone deserves another shot at happiness, it's you. Just don't get hurt. That heart of yours has been broken once.' Placing a hand on his chest, she lowered her eyes. 'It might not survive a second time.' Ben kissed Mary warmly on her cheek again and left.

CHAPTER ELEVEN

March 2015 – Grace sat on the settee shoehorned between two children watching yet another Disney film. A week had passed since she'd come to stay at Lucy's. After giving it lots of thought, in the early hours, when she'd been unable to sleep, she had decided today would be her last at her friend's. Not that she hadn't enjoyed the company of Lucy, Tim and their kids, it just seemed the right time to return home. The child to her left, a young girl, smiled at her. Grace brushed to the side the hair partly obscuring the girl's eyes.

'Where's your Mum?' Grace asked.

A younger boy to Grace's right tugged at her arm. 'She's in the garden with Daddy.'

'They're planning a barbeque,' the girl said. 'Daddy said I can have some of my friends from school.'

Grace stroked the girl's long hair. 'Who's your best friend?'

The girl sat upright. 'Well. It was Melissa Parkinson, but now I think it's Ruby.'

'What about you, Harry? Will you be inviting any friends?' She nudged the boy playfully.

'Only Tommy.' He answered, without looking away from the screen.

Grace leant forward. 'Who wants a drink?' Extricating herself from the children she stood and turned to face them.

'Me, Aunty Grace.' They shouted in unison.

Grace comically lowered her features into a scowl. 'No fighting while I'm away. Amy, Harry.'

Amy pulled a cushion from her side and plonked it between herself and her brother as if to establish no man's land. Harry stuck his tongue out at his sister, pulled a cushion from the side of him, and did likewise. Grace smiled. Realising she could trust the bellicose youngsters for a few moments, headed for the kitchen. She filled three glasses with orange cordial and water and placed them on the worktop near to the door. She peeped out into the garden. Bright sunshine draped itself across the lawn, stretching from one side before halting abruptly near to a brightly-coloured flowerbed still in the shade. She heard voices behind the garage and ambled outside. The warmth from the sun enveloping her as she stepped away from the cool interior of the kitchen. She strolled through the pergola and stopped as she heard her name mentioned. Lucy and Tim stood next to a large garden shed. Grace listened. Moving to the side behind a large shrub out of view of the pair. She crept closer.

Tim turned to face his wife. 'Lucy.' Holding out his arms. 'Grace can stay here as long as she wants. You know that.'

Grace peered between the branches of a tree. The conversation now within earshot.

'I know, it's just.' Lucy paused, glancing along the length of the garden towards the kitchen. 'I'm concerned about her.'

Tim followed her gaze. 'She seems much better. You said so yourself last night.'

'Grace hides her feelings. She bottles it up inside until it comes bursting out. She's always done that.'

'Isn't that most people?'

Lucy shook her head. 'No. Most people talk to friends and family. Grace ...'

'She'll have to come to terms with what happened eventually. Sorry to be blunt but that's the truth. I love Grace. She's good for you, but she's not a child. It was a tragic accident.'

'I'm worried she might ...'

Tim furrowed his brow and shook his head. 'You're not talking about ... suicide?' Fixing her with a stare as Lucy shrugged, her head dropping down.

Tim clasped hold of his wife's hand, gently tugging it to get her to look up. 'Grace is not the type. You worry about everything. Grace wouldn't—'

'How do you know?' Tears swamped her eyes. Her voice trembling.

Tim pulled his wife close. 'Hey.' Kissing the top of her head. 'Why don't you and Grace have a heart to heart this afternoon. I'll take the kids out somewhere. See if you can get her to open up. I'm sure you're worrying over nothing.'

'She's my best friend, Tim. We're like sisters. If anything happened to her, I'd be ...' Lucy shook her head, as if the word she desperately searched for didn't exist.

Grace crept out from behind her vantage point and slipped back towards the house. Glancing behind herself every couple of feet as she tiptoed back inside.

Grace went back to bed about ten. Her lack of sleep during the night and early hours of the morning having an enervating effect. She'd risen after lunch, showering and changing into jeans and t-shirt. She had even gone to the trouble of applying makeup, something she had neglected to do for days. She bounded downstairs striding through the lounge and dining room into the kitchen where Lucy was preparing a meal.

Grace smiled. 'Morning, again.'

'Afternoon actually. You seem chipper.' Lucy placed the lid on the casserole dish and turned to face her friend.

'I feel a lot better.'

'I'm doing a beef stew for tea.'

Grace hopped onto one of the two stools near the breakfast bar. 'Where's Tim and the kids?'

'He's taken them to the pictures.'

Grace stretched her arms towards the ceiling. 'That sleep did me a world of good. I feel refreshed.'

'What veg should I do? What would you prefer?'

'Look, Lucy.' Shuffling on her seat. 'I think it's about time I returned home. You and Tim have been wonderful, but I've imposed enough.'

Lucy edged closer. 'You don't have to. Tim and I—'

Grace smiled and held up a hand. 'I'm going for my sanity. There's only so many Disney movies a person can watch. If I sit through any more, I'll go Daffy Duck.'

'Daffy Duck was Looney Tunes.' Easing herself onto the other stool next to Grace.

Grace giggled. 'Only you would know that.'

Lucy took hold of Grace's hand. 'You don't need to go today though? I could take you home tomorrow.'

Grace pondered for a moment, tapping Lucy's hand. 'I think I may cope with one more day here.'

Lucy nodded. 'Ok. It's settled.'

Grace stretched forward and hugged her friend. 'I love you, Lucy Roberts. You do know that? You're special to me—'

'Grace—'

Grace held up a hand again. 'Let me finish, please. I don't tell you often enough how important you are. You've always been there for me. I'm so grateful. I'll get through this.' Gently shaking her friend's hands, she kissed her on the cheek. Lucy's eyes dropped down. Grace gently lifted her chin. 'I know you worry … about everything. I would never do anything stupid. Honest.'

Lucy pulled Grace towards her and hugged her tightly. 'Promise me. You bloody well swear it!' Her eyes glistened with tears.

'I promise.'

Lucy pulled the car up outside Grace's home, jumped out and opened the boot, allowing Grace to retrieve her bag. The two embraced.

She gazed into Grace's eyes. 'You will ring if you need anything?' Her eyes full of tears.

'Of course.' She handed her friend a tissue, pulled from her pocket. 'Look at you. I'll be fine.'

Grace prised herself from Lucy and trudged up the path to her flat. She stopped, smiled and waved at her friend. Lucy returned her wave, slipped back into her car and drove off. Grace inserted the key and pushed. The door making a scraping noise as it forced the post and magazines behind it. She closed the door and leant back against it. Her shoulders slumped as the realisation dawned on her, she was now alone. Alone with her thoughts. She closed her eyes and took a deep breath.

'Right young lady,' she mouthed. 'Time to move on.'

CHAPTER TWELVE

JUNE 2012 – Mary popped her head into the dining room. 'Ben. Can you give me a hand?' Ben strode into the kitchen, his sister held out a large plate with sausages, burgers and chicken drumsticks on it. 'Take these out to Toby will you?'

He nodded towards the garden. 'It's gorgeous out there.'

'I know, it makes a change. Generally, when we have a barbeque, it pisses down.' Mary gathered buns and bowls containing salad as she followed her brother outside.

People sat around the sun-drenched garden. Some on deck chairs, others perched on large plant containers, chatting pleasantly. Every now and again laughter erupted amongst the guests. Ben stopped next to his brother-in-law who stood behind the barbeque. His apron complete with the nude body of a woman on the front, and his oversized chef's hat, giving him a comical appearance.

'Thanks, Ben.' Taking the plate of meat from him, he began to arrange them on the grill.

Ben smiled and nodded at Toby. 'Love the apron. Suits you.'

'Mary bought it for me. She knows me so well your sister.'

'Ben,' Mary said. Motioning for him to join her. 'Have you met Mel?'

'No, I don't think I have.' Wandering over he smiled at the attractive blonde woman stood with his sister.

She smiled at him. 'Hi.' Holding out a hand which Ben shook.

Mary winked at Ben. 'Can you two excuse me? I have to check on my wedges.'

Ben and Mel watched as Mary made her way back in the house. Mel turned to face Ben. 'I think that was a clumsy attempt at matchmaking, don't you?'

'Yeah. That's my sister. Always trying to palm me off on someone … I didn't mean … no offence …'

She smiled. 'It's ok. None taken.'

'Mel? Short for?'

'Melanie. And Ben? Short for Benjamen, I suppose?'

'Yeah.' He smiled at her. 'Can I get you a drink?'

'Yes, please. I'm parched.'

'Lager, beer, quadruple whisky?'

She laughed. 'All of those. But maybe a glass of prosecco to begin with.'

Ben opened the fridge in the kitchen and pulled out two bottles of lager. He turned as Mary entered, his sister raising her eyebrows. 'You and Mel appear to be getting along well.'

He rolled his eyes. 'After your pathetic matchmaking attempt.'

'I don't know what you're on about, Bennie-boy. Two lagers?' Nodding at the bottles.

'One's for Toby. Got to keep the Chef happy.'

Mary leant against the worktop. 'She's divorced you know.'

Ben lowered his eyebrows. 'Who?'

'Mel. She's a catch.'

He sighed. 'Mary.' Staring at his sister. 'I don't need any help in that department.'

'I'm just saying that's all. She got a huge settlement from her ex.'

'So?'

'Don't you fancy being a kept man? You can hang up your saw for good.'

'Not really. Anyway. Why did she get divorced?'

Mary pouted and threw out her hands. 'Her husband was shagging his secretary. I mean, how cliched is that?'

'Very.' He turned to leave.

'She's probably gagging for it as well.' Grinned Mary as Ben swung back around.

'I'll tell Mel what you said.'

'Don't you dare. She'd never speak to me again.'

'Anyway. How do you know she's gagging for it? As you elegantly put it.'

'She told me. She hasn't slept with anyone since her husband. Eighteen months ago.'

'Thanks for sharing that. She's lovely Mary, but I'm not interested in anyone at the moment.'

Mary raised her eyebrows. 'What about you? It must be a while since you …'

'I'm not standing here discussing my sex life with my sister.'

'There was a time, Bennie-boy, when you would tell your big sister everything.'

'There are some things I keep to myself.' Ben smiled.

Ben's mobile sounded. He put the beers on the worktop and pulled it from his jeans back pocket, viewing a number he didn't recognise. 'Ben Stainton,' he said.

'Hi, Ben. It's Sarah. Sarah Williams from Wynyard. I don't know if you remember me?'

'Of course I remember you.' A grin spread across his face.

Mary scrutinised him. Ben turned away from his sister. 'What can I do for you?'

'I was tidying the other day when I found a tool of yours. A plane.'

'Oh, yes. I am missing one. I've been wracking my brains where I put it. It belonged to my dad. It has sentimental value.'

'Well, I'll keep it here for you. If you'd like to pop around and pick it up.'

'Thanks. When would be best?' Ben said.

'Monday. Around lunch-time.'

'I'll see you then.'

'Ok,' Sarah said.

Ben turned and eyed his sister who stood with her arms folded. He smiled at her. 'What?'

Mary raised her eyebrows. 'Sarah? Sarah from Wynyard? Married, unhappy Sarah?'

'What if it was?' Picking the bottles back up, he turned away from her.

'Mel will be disappointed.'

'If she has so much money, and she really is gagging for it, she could always rent a stud,' he said over his shoulder.

Ben pulled up outside Sarah's house in Wynyard. Getting out he marched towards the door which opened before he reached it. Sarah stood there. Her hair hung loosely instead of the pony-tail she typically wore. Her face ordinarily devoid of make-up had just the right amount on. She smiled at Ben. A warm, welcoming smile.

'Hi,' she said. And moved aside to allow Ben to step indoors.

'How are you?' Ben said.

'Good.' Motioning for him to go into the dining room. 'I made some lunch.'

'Thanks.' He removed his jacket and placed it on the back of a chair. 'I was hoping you would.'

'Drink?' Sarah said.

'Just juice. I've got to go and price a job later. It wouldn't be professional to arrive smelling of beer.'

'Juice it is.' She disappeared into the kitchen for a few moments before she returned with two glasses.

'Orange ok?' she said.

Ben nodded and took the drink from her.

They chatted as they ate. Ben recounting funny stories about jobs he'd carried out in the past. Sarah listened intently to him. Any time the conversation appeared to flag, she would ask him a question or two, and Ben would eagerly answer.

'You said the plane belonged to your dad?'

'Yeah. He was a carpenter too.'

'I think you mentioned that previously.' Leaning closer to him.

Ben smiled at her. 'You've a good memory.'

'Only for certain things. Is your dad ...'

'Yeah. I had a rough time that year. I lost Dad and then Katherine.'

'Your wife?'

'Yeah.'

'I'm sorry.' Placing her hand on top of his. 'Tell me about her?'

'Childhood sweethearts.' Ben smiled. 'She was a year below me at school. We met when I was fifteen, and she was fourteen. The funny thing was, only a couple of months separated us. My birthday's in August, and hers is ... was ... September. We started going out soon after.'

Sarah removed her hand from his. 'How did she die?'

'Breast cancer.'

'I see.' Replacing her hand, she gently squeezed his. 'Have you any children?'

'No. We were planning to, but ...'

'It must have been hard? Losing her so young?'

'It was, but you battle through. I've a good family. My sister, Mary, was brilliant. It's because we're twins. We have this special bond. That's what she says.'

'I didn't know you're a twin.' Sarah stood and collected the plates.

'You didn't ask.'

Ben watched as she disappeared with the pots and empty glasses. He glanced around the grand dining room. Suddenly, he felt guilty for being with Sarah. She was married after all. How would he feel if his wife was having a meal with another man while he was at work? He shouldn't be here. Maybe he should have just collected the plane and left. He could have declined the offer of a meal. But in truth he liked Sarah. He wanted to come. He loved talking to her. She listened to him. She cared, or appeared to. His thoughts interrupted by Sarah returning with fresh drinks.

'I've got us another drink.' Holding out a glass to him.

'I should get going.' Ben rose from his seat.

'Oh ... of course. You told me you had a job to go to.'

She followed Ben into the hall as he made his way towards the door.

She stopped and held up her hand. 'Your plane.' Heading into the garage and returning moments later. Moving across to Ben she held it out. Her hand trembling slightly as he took it from her.

'Thanks for the meal and chat,' he said. 'I really enjoyed today.'

'Did you?' Gazing deeply into his eyes, she blushed. 'I've a confession. I'm sorry.'

'What for?'

'I hid the plane. I removed it from your tool bag and kept it here. I wanted to see you again.' She looked towards the floor. 'I know it was wrong but ...'

Ben stepped closer and lifted her chin with his hand. 'I forgive you.' Allowing his hand to slide around from her chin to her cheek as Sarah brought her hand up and placed it on top of his.

'You're beautiful.' He found himself saying rather than thinking.

'Am I?' Staring into his eyes. Slowly Ben lowered his lips to hers. The touch a soft and gentle meeting. Sarah closed her eyes as Ben pressed harder. He pulled her closer, and Sarah winced.

'What's up?' he said, as Sarah backed away.

'I banged my side the other day.' Glancing away from him. 'It's still a little tender.'

'I'm sorry ... I didn't mean to ...'

She stepped forward and touched his hand. 'You've nothing to be sorry for. I ...' Sarah stopped mid-sentence as a car pulled onto the drive. She raced towards the door and opened it as Aaron jumped out of his vehicle. He stared first at Ben and then Sarah as he marched towards the house.

'Ben left a plane here last week,' Sarah said. 'He was passing and popped by to collect it.'

'I see.' Walking past Ben, he turned and smiled. 'You did a cracking job on my study.'

'Glad you like it.' Ben turned towards Sarah. 'Thanks again, Mrs Williams.' Holding up the tool he forced a smile. 'It was my dad's.'

'Sentimental?' Aaron said.

'Yeah.'

'It's terrible when you lose something that's yours.' Staring directly at Ben, he curled his lip. 'Or someone takes it from you.'

'It is.' Moving outside towards his van, he opened the door and stepped in allowing himself a final look at Sarah. She stood at the threshold, her husband's arm draped protectively across her shoulder. Her eyes peeked up from the ground for the briefest of moments at Ben. The smiling, happy face from earlier no longer there.

After pricing up a job near Durham, Ben travelled home. He placed his van keys on the coffee table in the lounge and threw his coat onto a chair. He changed. Pulling on a pair of jogging pants and a t-shirt. Ben perched on the edge of the bed and put on his trainers. He gazed at the photograph on the bedside cabinet. The picture frame glass covered in dust. He picked it up and using the bottom of his t-shirt wiped it clean. The attractive, smiling face of his wife stared at him. He studied the photo as he'd done countless times before putting it back. Getting up he trudged towards the door and glanced back at the picture again. He turned, picked up the house keys, and went for a run.

Ben returned from his jog, showered, dressing in jeans and a t-shirt, and slumped into a seat. Picking up his mobile he searched his contacts.

'Hello?' said a male voice on the other end.

'Stan. It's Ben.'

'Ben. How are you?'

'I'm well.' Ben said.

'Family ok?'

'They are. What about your brood?' Ben asked.

Stan laughed. 'Still mad. But in a good way.'

'Are you busy?'

'Not at the moment. Sheila's gone out with the girls, and I was doing a spot of gardening. Contemplating treating myself to a pint. I think I've earned one.'

'I could do with a chat,' Ben said.

'Yeah. Of course.'

'I'll come across to you. Buy you that pint.'

Stan chuckled. 'Now you're talking.'

Ben paid the taxi driver and headed into the pub. Stan stood at the bar, turning as Ben entered.

Stan held out his hand. 'Hi, big fella.'

'Nice to see you.' Shaking Stan's hand while warmly patting his friend on the arm.

'Grab those seats in the corner,' Stan said. 'I'll get us a drink.'

Ben pulled a note from his jeans and handed the money to his friend. 'My treat.' And headed for the table.

Stan paid for the drinks, and picking up the pints joined Ben. He placed the glasses down along with the change and lowered himself into the seat opposite. 'So.' Taking a large swig from his beer. 'What's up?'

Ben smiled. 'Is it that obvious?'

'Yep. It is.'

Ben gulped at his pint cradling the half-empty glass in his hands. He leant forward in his seat. 'I've met someone. Someone I like very much.'

'That's great.' Patting the arm of his friend. 'How long is it ... since Katherine?'

'Ten years.' Ben shuffled in his seat. 'When you lost Pam ...'

Stan leant back in his chair rubbing his grey beard. 'I see. You're feeling guilty.'

'It's that obvious?'

'When Pam died I thought my life was over. At least that part of it. The counselling helped greatly of course. Meeting people like you who'd experienced the same thing as me, got me through it. Pam and I had a wonderful marriage. She was my soul-mate. I didn't believe I could feel the same way about another woman. Then Sheila came along.'

Ben drained his pint. 'Did you feel guilty?'

'Of course. It's only natural,' Stan said. 'You need to move on with your life. Pam would never have wanted me to go on mourning her forever. She loved me. Katherine would be the same I'm sure.'

'It's just ...' Ben paused and placed his empty glass down. 'It feels like a betrayal.'

'I know. But it's not. I often think of Pam. A smell or a sound throws open a window to my past. I can't do anything about that. But I love Sheila. You can find another soul-mate. If you search hard enough.'

'Doesn't it devalue what you had with Pam though?'

'Not a bit. I look at it like this. I had a life when Pam was here and another when she was gone. What's the alternative? Living a sad, lonely existence. Wandering around an empty house. The six years Sheila and I have been together have been some of the happiest of my life.'

Ben rubbed his chin. 'Katherine's things. Photos, clothes, jewellery. I've kept them all. I'm not sure I could ...'

Stan leant in closer placing a hand on Ben's shoulder. 'I won't kid you. It wasn't easy. But when the time came, I boxed everything and put them away until the day I was ready to part with them for good. The trinkets and other things I gave to the girls. It's memories that matter not stuff.'

'Sarah,' Ben said. 'She's called Sarah.'

Stan smiled. 'Am I going to meet this Sarah?'

'It's not straightforward. She's married.'

Stan leant back in his chair. 'Right. I see. That's a little more complicated.'

'She's desperately unhappy.'

'Has she told you this?'

'No. I can sense it. Sarah appears ...' Ben thought hard. 'Her husband seems to dominate her. It's as if she's afraid of him.'

'So you've met her husband?'

'I did work at their house.'

'Could you have misread the signals? Maybe she was being nice.'

Ben shook his head. 'It wasn't like that.'

Stan nodded. 'Why doesn't she leave him? If she's unhappy. It isn't like years ago when women had no one to help them.'

Ben shrugged. 'She has no family up here. I think she's on her own. Maybe it's too daunting for her. To go it alone I mean.'

Stan leant forward again. 'Ask her. Find out if her marriage is unhappy. If it's not …'

'I know. I did think about that. When I was at her house today, I felt guilty for being there. We ate lunch together and chatted, that's all. But there's something not right.'

'You think he hits her?'

'I don't know. It's just this feeling. There's something about him I don't like. What if he is? What if I make things worse for her?'

Stan stood, picking up the empty glasses. 'If he's abusing her she needs to leave him. I'll get us another pint. Plan our next move.'

'Sorry to burden you with my troubles.'

Stan patted Ben on the arm. 'Don't be daft. What are friends for?'

Ben pulled his van up a short distance from Sarah's house. He could clearly see from his vantage point the driveway was empty. He picked up his mobile and rang.

'Hello,' Sarah whispered.

'Sarah. It's Ben. How are you?'

'Ben. I'm … Ok.'

'I was thinking of popping around … for a chat.'

'Oh … It's not really a good time ... I've family visiting.'

'I see,' Ben said.

'Maybe another time.'

'Yeah. No problem.'

'Ben,' Sarah said. 'Thanks.'

'Thanks? What for?'

'Just thanks.'

She hung up and Ben stared at his mobile, a deep frown etched on his face.

June 15th, 2012 – I plucked up the courage and phoned Ben today. I lied about the plane. He's coming around to collect it on Monday. I'm counting the minutes. I just had to see him again. Is he the one who'll save me from this hell? I'm dying a little each day I spend here.

June 17th, 2012 – Aaron came home unexpectedly while Ben was here. I tried to placate him, but he was livid calling me a whore and a slag. He no longer seems bothered that my bruises are visible. I actually took the tablets out of the box and held them in my hand. Death seemed so welcoming, and I'm sure I would have swallowed them had Ben not phoned. I remembered our kiss and stepped back from the abyss. He wanted to visit, but I put him off. I can't let him see me like this. I feel so ashamed.

June 18th, 2012 – Aaron was still angry. He searched through my stuff looking for evidence of my infidelity. Luckily my journals are well hidden. He left in a rage. I'm dreading his return.

June 19th, 2012 – Spent the day in bed curled up in a ball. I can't look at myself in the mirror. The bruises mean nothing now. I don't even feel the pain anymore. I'm dying from the inside out. If it wasn't for Ben, I'd leave this life. Aaron has almost won. I'm just another object he owns, another possession he doesn't want but refuses to relinquish.

June 20th, 2012 – I've decided to risk everything. I'm aware this could be my final entry in my journal. I'm hoping Lady-Luck will shine on me today. Leave tonight, or live and die this way.

CHAPTER THIRTEEN

Ben sat reading a newspaper in his flat. The remnants of his breakfast scattered across the table in front of him. Sipping his tea, he glanced at the clock on the wall. He was due to begin a new job today for a customer not too far from where he lived. Satisfied he still had a little time, he resumed his reading. His phone sounded. Ben folded the paper and dropped it onto the seat next to him stretching across the table to pick up his mobile.

'Hello.' The number unfamiliar.

'Ben? It's Margaret Hughes. From the Grove.'

'Hi there,' Ben said.

'Sorry to bugger you about, Ben, but somethings come up. I have to travel to Leeds. Could we put the job back until next week? I'm sorry about this.'

'No that's fine. I've got other stuff to be getting on with at my workshop. I'll give you a call later in the week to discuss what days are best for you.'

'Thanks,' she said.

Ben's phone beeped, indicating someone else was trying to get through. He viewed the phone. The name Sarah on the screen. 'I'm going to have to go, Margaret. I've another call. We'll speak later.'

'No problem. Bye,' she said.

Ben quickly accepted Sarah's call. 'Hi.'

'Ben,' she said, so quietly he struggled to hear her. 'Please come.'

'Sarah?' he said.

The phone went dead. He searched his mobile for her number and returned the call. The phone rang out for several moments before switching to answer-phone. He leapt up and threw on his coat. Thrusting his mobile into his pocket, he raced towards the door. Collecting his van keys, he hurried outside, jumped in his van, and roared off.

Ben pulled his car onto the drive of Sarah's house screeching to a halt outside the building. Not even bothering to shut the door to his van he raced towards the house. He reached for the handle and paused, the door to the property slightly ajar. He pushed it open and peered into the hall. The pictures which once adorned the walls now shattered on the floor. Glass and debris lay everywhere. He tiptoed forward, the crunch of his boots on broken glass the only sound in the eerie silence.

'Sarah,' he shouted. His voice reverberating around the emptiness of the room. Listening as deafening silence echoed back. He wandered on into the dining room, the usual pristine interior now a scene of utter devastation. Upturned chairs lay on their backs. One with a broken leg resting at the foot of the fireplace, the cracked mirror above hanging precariously from the wall. Carrying on into the kitchen he gasped. The drawers of units open, their contents now littering the floor. Broken plates and glass lay everywhere. Knives, forks, spoons and other assorted cutlery scattered about. Ben gulped in air, his heart-rate quickening further. As his thoughts turned to Sarah, he moved swiftly back into the dining room and into the hall. He mounted the stairs two at a time bursting into the first room he reached. It was a bathroom. Or what remained of it. The contents of cupboards, seemingly thrown against the wall, lay on the bottom of the bath in a sickly heap. One thing struck him straight away. The lotions and perfumes. The deodorants, shampoos and everything else was feminine. There didn't appear as if anything belonged to a man. Ben turned and stepped onto the landing.

'Sarah!' His voice now quivering. He heard a sound to his left. A shuffle of someone or something moving inside one of the other rooms. He crept towards the door and pushed it open. Sarah lay half upright against the far wall. His eyes momentarily drawn towards one of the pillows on the bed. A red smudge marring it's otherwise pristine whiteness.

He stared back at her. 'Sarah,' he whispered. 'It's Ben.'

She slowly lifted her head and looked vacantly at him. Ben manoeuvred around the bed and dropped to his knees as she turned full on to face him.

He sucked in a lungful of air. Sarah's face almost unrecognisable. Her top lip split, blood seeping from the wound. Her right eye swollen horribly. Dry blood covered the other half of her face where she'd evidently lain. He reached out his huge right hand allowing it to gently cup her chin. Sarah opened her left eye, her right almost entirely shut. She forced a smile at him. Her facial injuries making a mockery of her attempt.

'I knew you'd come,' she whispered.

'What happened?' His mind struggling to take in the devastation of her once flawless features.

'Aaron came home. He was so angry. He found the box you made for me.'

'He did this?' Anger erupting within him. He fought to suppress it. 'Can you stand?'

Sarah nodded. Ben assisted Sarah to her feet. She winced from unseen injuries as he helped her from the floor and lowered her onto the bed.

He scanned the room. 'I'll call someone.'

'Please don't.' Her head dropped to her chest. Her shoulders hunched.

Ben stared back at her. 'But—'

'He didn't find them. I hid them well.'

'Find what?' Assisting Sarah as she struggled to stand again.

Sarah stared around the room. Her eyes surveying the mess of ripped clothing strewn across the floor.

She dropped to her knees. 'My necklace.' Looking up at him. Tears now swamping her eyes. 'The Dove.'

He squatted down and placed an arm around her. 'It wasn't expensive. We can buy another.' Brushing the bloodied hair from her face.

She peered deep into his eyes. 'Please. It's important to me.' Ben shook his head but helped her search. Sarah frantically throwing clothing from the floor onto the bed.

Ben jumped up. 'Here it is.' Holding the silver dove between his thumb and index finger.

Sarah shuffled across to him and tentatively took hold of it. 'He snapped the chain,' she said. Staring at Ben, tears rolling from her left eye. Her right now fully closed.

He cupped her chin again. 'Don't worry about the chain. We can get another.' He scanned the room, taking in the carnage and shook his head. 'You can't stay here. He's trashed the place.'

Sarah staggered towards the door. Ben took hold of her arm and assisted her as she limped downstairs. He frowned, puzzled by where she was leading him. They reached the bottom, Sarah quickened her stride and burst into her Aaron's den. She stopped and brought a hand to her mouth muffling the sob escaping her lips. Dropping to her knees, she stared at the unit Ben constructed for her husband. The front smashed. The doors and drawers shattered into pieces. The culprit, an axe, lay on the floor. Sarah began to sob her shoulders shuddering as her crying intensified.

Ben dropped down onto his knees next to her. He gently turned her face towards him, and brushed some stray hairs from her eyes. 'What's wrong?' His hand resting lightly on her cheek.

'Look at what he's done. All your wonderful work—'

He pulled her close. 'It's wood, that's all. I can easily make another. You're more important.' Kissing the top of her head, he hugged her close. 'A piece of furniture doesn't matter.'

Sarah pulled her head away from him. 'I'm sorry for involving you in this.'

Ben gently stroked her hair. 'Don't be stupid.' His eyes now swamped with tears. He kissed her head again, gently rocking her as she continued to sob. He held her like this until her crying subsided.

Finally prising herself away from him she limped to the corner of the room where a leather chair sat. Pushing it away she ripped the carpet from the skirting-board. Below she tugged at a piece of loose floorboard and lifted this. Sarah reached inside and pulled out something. She turned to show Ben the books she now held tightly. 'My journals,' she whispered. As if this explanation was enough. 'I was smart. I hid them in the one place he wouldn't think of looking. His den.' Sarah clambered to her feet and hobbled across to Ben, her head drooped. 'I couldn't leave them. There's part of me inside these.' Clutching the books tightly to her chest.

'Have you a suitcase or a bag?' Ben said.

'In the garage.'

'Let's collect some of your clothing. What's left of it.'

'I haven't anywhere—'

'Don't worry about that.' He bent and gently kissed her cheek. 'Come on.' Motioning towards the door.

Ben, carrying a holdall, led Sarah into the hall and stopped as a vehicle pulled up outside. Motioning for her to halt, he put a finger to his lips. 'Wait here.' Dropping the bag onto the floor, he raced towards the door and peered through the glass. It was Aaron. Ben snarled, grasping the handle he threw open the door. Aaron halted in his tracks and stared at Ben who stepped outside, a scowl filling his face.

Aaron sneered. 'What the hell are you doing here?'

Ben launched himself at Aaron, crashing into him. The pair careering onto the bonnet of Aaron's car before slipping off the side and dropping to the floor. He was quick to his feet, and as the younger man turned to face him, Ben struck him forcefully on his jaw. Aaron fell backwards, momentarily stunned by the blow. He shook his head and put a hand to his mouth, blood running from one side of it. Ben turned on hearing footsteps behind him. Sarah stood at the threshold. She gasped and brought her hands up to her face.

Ben held out a hand. 'Stay there,' he said. And spun back to face the now upright Aaron. Aaron staggered around to the boot of his car and flung it open. Pulling a golf club from inside he slammed it shut again. Manoeuvring around the car, he edged towards Ben swinging the club wildly. Raising the would-be weapon, he launched himself at Ben. The older man anticipating his movement met him half-way and caught Aaron in a perfectly timed rugby tackle. The two combatants skidded to a halt on the gravel. Ben jumped to his feet, towering above Aaron, pulling back his fist as the younger man used his foot to push Ben away. Ben stumbled backwards losing his footing as Aaron sprung to his feet and dived into his car. The engine roared into life. Ben, suspecting what Aaron intended to do, rolled out of the path of the vehicle. Aaron reversed stopping inches from the wall. Ben up in a flash, raced around to the driver's side, pulled at the now locked door handle and banged on the glass. Aaron struggled to find first gear as Ben, his anger intensifying further, thumped harder on the side window. Aaron's eye's widened as he viewed the irate Ben through the glass. Ben thumped again. Pulling his fist back he smashed it into the window. Glass shattered over Aaron, who ducked instinctively throwing out a defensive arm that caught Ben on the side of his face. The bigger man stumbled and Aaron finally locating first-gear tried to move. The wheels struggled to gain traction on the loose gravel surface as Ben made a grab for him, wrapping an arm around Aaron. The car leapt forward and Ben, still holding on to Aaron, was taken off his feet.

Sarah screamed. 'Ben!' The car shot out of the drive with Ben still attached. Ben pulled on the steering wheel as the two men fought for outright control. The vehicle skidded, then careered over the footpath and into a tree. Ben, who was thrown from it, put a hand to his head. Momentarily dazed he stared across at the car with it's front now crumpled. It reversed back onto the tarmac and shot forward along the road. Ben got to his feet and roared. His heart jackhammering in his chest. He turned as Sarah came hobbling from the drive. She hurried to him and throwing her arms around his massive frame, hugged him.

'I thought he was going to kill you,' Sarah said.

'I'm all right.' Lifting up her face from his chest, he kissed her. 'I'm ok.'

He led her back towards his van and helped her into the passenger seat. Racing indoors he returned with the bag and threw it into the back. Ben took out his mobile, the screen now cracked, and texted. Starting the engine he reversed, performing a turn in the large drive. He stopped at the threshold of the road as a car sped past. Ben smiled at Sarah and placing his hand on hers, lightly squeezed.

Sarah gently took hold of Ben's blood-covered left hand. 'You're injured.'

He put his other hand to her cheek. 'I'm fine. Don't worry about me.'

Tears tumbled down her face. 'Thanks … for coming.'

He smiled at her, gently tapping her hand. 'You're safe now.' And drove off.

Ben leapt up from his seat as the bell to his flat sounded. He raced towards the front door, closing the one to the lounge behind him. Peering through the glass, he pulled it open.

Mary stood outside in her nurse's uniform. 'What's up?' she said, stepping inside.

'It's Sarah.' Taking hold of his sister's arm, he led her towards the lounge. 'Her husband has attacked her. Will you check her over?'

'Of course.' Putting a hand on his arm, she viewed the tears in her brother's eyes. 'Are you ok?'

Ben forced a smile. 'Yeah.' Turning as Mary followed him into the lounge. 'Sarah. This is Mary, my sister. She's going to check you over. If that's all right.' Sarah nodded.

Mary raised her eyebrows at her brother. 'A bit of privacy.'

Ben smiled at Sarah and turned to leave. 'I'll make some drinks,' he said. Closing the door behind him.

Mary came into the kitchen and looked at Ben staring vacantly outside.

She blew out hard. 'I've checked her out. I think it might be wise to take her to the hospital. As a precaution. She has a nasty bump on her head and a lot of bruising.'

Ben brought his hands to his face. 'How could someone do that?' He turned and looked at his sister. 'She's so small, and he's nearly as tall as me.'

Mary edged closer. 'I don't know.' Shaking her head. 'She told me she doesn't want to go to the hospital. But if you ask, she might.'

'I could have killed him, Mary. I wanted to. I really did. I've never felt such rage. I should have seen what was happening earlier. I could have stopped this.' Turning away from his sister he resumed staring outside.

Mary moved forward and placed an arm around her brother. 'You saved her. She's safe now. Let's take her to accident and emergency. Just to be certain.' Ben nodded. 'Let me see your hand,' she said, holding out hers. She tutted taking hold of his bloodied and swollen hand. 'Can you bend your fingers?'.

'No.'

'I think it's broken,' she said, gently patting Ben's cheek.

He forced a passable smile and shrugged. 'I was due a few weeks holiday anyway.'

'Looks like you've got your wish.'

Ben strode along the corridor and into the ward as Mary exited one of the rooms. She stopped outside looking down at his newly plastered hand hanging by his side.

'How is she?' Ben asked.

'Fine. They're keeping her in overnight as a precaution. There's nothing serious though.'

'Can I see her?'

Mary smiled and placed a hand on her brother's arm. 'Of course. I'll meet you at the coffee shop downstairs.'

Ben hugged and kissed his sister and went inside.

June 21st 2012 – *I'm in the hospital overnight for observation. Ben convinced me it's for the best. I met his sister, Mary, today. I like her very much.*

June 22nd, 2012 – *Didn't sleep well. I woke up in a sweat. For a moment I thought I was back at Wynyard. Ben's coming this morning. I'm counting the seconds, minutes and hours until he arrives. Is Ben doing this because he pities me? What does my future hold?*

June 23rd, 2012 – *Ben came and collected me. He brought me flowers and insisted I stay at his flat. I feel incredibly lucky.*

I watched the sun rise in my sky today,
It's golden glow touched the blue within my soul,
I raised my head from darkest depths,
And felt the warmth envelop me,
I gazed into it's deepest eyes,
And found what I'd been searching for,
then,
I stretched my wings for a distant shore,
I've christened it and named it Ben.

Ben opened the front door of his flat. Two people stood outside. A plain-clothed policeman and a uniformed female officer. Ben beckoned them inside. They followed him into the lounge. Sarah glanced at the officers and forced a smile at Ben.

'Hello, Sarah,' the man said. 'I'm Detective Sergeant John Smith, and this is my colleague, Detective Constable Brenda Walker. Brenda will be your liaison officer.' Sarah nodded at the two officers who positioned themselves opposite.

Ben stepped towards the door. 'I'll make some tea.'

Sarah's eyes darted between Ben and the officers. 'Would it be all right if Ben stayed.' Her eyes now fixed on them. 'I'd really like him to if that's ok?'

The sergeant smiled at Sarah. 'Of course.'

Ben eased onto the settee next to Sarah. Taking hold of her hand, he gently squeezed it.

'In your own time, Sarah,' the Sergeant said.

Ben deep in thought was shaken from his reverie as the doorbell chimed. He marched off to answer it. Mary stood outside with Toby. Ben moved aside and allowed them to enter.

Mary patted Ben on the arm. 'Have they been?'

'They've just gone. I was going to make coffee. If you'd like some?'

'Yeah.' Mary said. She and Toby followed Ben into the kitchen. 'Where's Sarah?'

'She's sleeping. It was a bit of an ordeal for her.' Turning away from his sister he stared upwards and sucked in air.

Mary motioned towards Toby who took the hint and carried on making the drinks. Ben's shoulders slumped as he looked outside into the yard. Mary stepped forward and put her arm around his shoulder. 'How are you?' she said.

He shrugged. 'Fine.'

'Sure?'

He gritted his teeth. 'I'm fine. I wasn't the one battered black and blue. I wasn't the one physically and sexually abused by that bastard. It was going on for years, Mary.' His eyes now awash with tears.

She placed an arm around him. 'It's over now though. Let the police deal with it.'

'I should have killed him.' Turning to look directly at his sister. 'I'd gladly do time for it.'

June 24th, 2012 – The police came to interview me today. I told them everything. Ben sat with me and held my hand throughout. I don't want secrets between us, I felt he should know everything. His touch gave me the strength to relive the ordeal. Strange. It's as if it happened to someone else.

June 25th, 2012 – Ben's sister, Mary, brought some bits and pieces for me to wear. I'm so grateful to everyone. I fear losing Ben. When he holds me, it's as if time stands still. When I'm not in his arms, I feel empty. I wish, I wish, I wish…

Ben headed from the lounge into the hall of his flat and opened the front door. Two men stood outside.

'Benjamin Stainton?' said the elder of the two.

'Yeah.'

The two men held out their police credentials. 'I'm Detective Sergeant Welsh, and this is my colleague Detective Constable Hope. Can we come in for a chat?'

Ben stepped aside. 'Of course.' Closing the door, he led the officers into the lounge. Sarah who'd been watching television stared over at them.

'It's the police.' Indicating for them to sit.

'Is this about Aaron?' Sarah said.

'Yes,' Welsh said. 'You must be Sarah Williams?' Sarah nodded.

'Your husband has made a complaint,' Welsh continued.

Sarah crossed her arms. ' A complaint. I don't understand.'

Ben took hold of Sarah's hand. 'What sort of complaint?' he said.

Welsh glanced at Ben then back at Sarah. 'Assault.'

Ben sneered. 'Assault. Can you see what he did to Sarah?'

'I'm aware Mrs Williams is pursuing a case of assault against her husband. I've spoken at length with my colleagues, but—'

'But nothing,' Sarah said. 'Ben was only protecting me.'

'I know this is difficult,' Welsh said. 'But it's a serious charge he's made, and we do have to investigate it.'

Ben patted Sarah on her arm. 'What did he say?'

Hope opened a notebook. 'He claims you assaulted him on his own property. He said he came home and you attacked him causing several injuries. A fractured cheekbone, two broken ribs and the loss of two teeth.'

Sarah looked up at Ben and then back to the officers. 'This is ridiculous. Aaron tried to run Ben over.'

'We have a witness,' Welsh said. 'A neighbour. He claims he heard a commotion outside, and when he looked, he saw a man attacking Mr Williams through his car window. He said it appeared Mr Williams was trying to escape from this man.'

Ben sighed. 'We fought. I don't deny that.'

Welsh stared at Ben's injured hand. 'Did you attack Mr Williams?'

'I was angry. I saw what he'd done to Sarah, and I went for him.'

'Mr Williams claims you and his wife have been conducting an affair behind his back, he—'

Sarah picked up a tissue from the arm of the chair and blew her nose. 'That's rubbish.' Her eyes now full of tears. 'Ben and I are just good friends.'

The two policemen glanced at each other. Hope flicked over the page in his book. 'You see how it appears? You husband came home early and found his wife with another man.'

Ben shook his head slowly. 'That's not how it happened. Sarah phoned me. Her husband assaulted her, and she rang me. I went around there and found her in a terrible state. We were leaving when he came home.'

'And you admit assaulting Mr Williams?'

'Yes … but it's not that straight-forward.'

96

'How long have you two known each other?' Welsh asked.

'A few weeks,' Sarah whispered.

The two policemen glanced at each other again.

'Why didn't you telephone the police?' Hope said. 'Or someone else? A friend or family perhaps.'

'I don't have anyone else. Ben's my friend. I was frightened Aaron would come back.'

Welsh stood. 'These are serious charges, Mr Stainton. We'd like you to come down to the station and give a statement.' He motioned towards the door as Hope joined his superior.

'Now?'

'Yes now,' Welsh said.

Hope closed his notebook and studied Ben and Sarah. 'It might be a good idea if Mrs Williams came too. So we can obtain her side of the story.'

Ben came out of the interview room. Escorted to reception by a constable where Sarah and Mary were waiting for him. The trio made their way outside and into Toby's car. Mary sat in the front. Ben and Sarah squeezed into the rear.

Mary swivelled around facing Ben and Sarah. 'What did they say?'

Ben sighed. 'The police released me on bail. I've been charged.'

'But how can they do that?' Sarah said. 'You didn't do anything wrong.'

'That's not how they see it. And with one of the neighbours corroborating Aaron's version of events, the police don't have a choice.'

Toby turned around. 'So what did your solicitor say?'

'He said if Aaron proceeds with the allegations it'll probably end up in court.'

Sarah dropped her eyes to the floor. 'He will.'

Mary looked at Ben and then her husband. 'What if he's found guilty?'

Toby exhaled. 'Don't know. Suspended sentence probably. It depends on how the court views it.'

Sarah gently tugged Ben's arm. 'But what about what he did to me? Ben saved me. This isn't fair.'

Ben shrugged. 'I asked about that. My solicitor said it may help my case, but then again courts don't like people taking things into their own hands.'

Sarah took hold of Ben's uninjured hand. 'Oh Ben. I'm so sorry about this.' She tightly squeezed his hand, brought it to her lips, and kissed it.

He smiled at her. 'Let's not worry about it at the moment.' Squeezing Sarah's hand back.

Mary tapped the dashboard. 'You two are coming to ours. No excuses. I'll make us lunch.'

Ben was in the kitchen preparing breakfast as Sarah showered and changed. Closing the door to the bedroom, she picked up the telephone, dialled a number, and waited.

'Smithy, Jones and Johnson Solicitors,' a female voice said.

'Can you put me through to Mr Jones please?'

'Can I ask who's calling?'

'Sarah Williams.'

'I'll check if he's available.'

Sarah stood and opened the bedroom door glancing towards Ben, who was occupied in the kitchen. Satisfied, she shut the door and dropped onto the edge of the bed.

'Sarah,' said a male voice. 'How are you?'

'Fine. Thanks for taking my call, Gareth.'

'No problem. I guess this is about Ben Stainton?'

She swapped the phone to her other ear. 'It is. Why is Aaron doing this?'

'I think you know why. With you pressing charges against him, Aaron feels he has no choice.'

'But this isn't fair to Ben. He was only protecting me.'

'Cards on the table, Sarah. Aaron employs me. He has told me to pursue this with the utmost vigour. He is willing to push this as far as he can. He's adamant he wants a conviction. If I'm honest, your friend will be fortunate not to end up in prison over this.'

Sarah sighed. 'What if I drop the charges against him?'

'Would you like me to ask Aaron?'

'Tell him if he drops his allegations against Ben, I'll get the police to drop the charges against him.'

'Are you sure you want to do this?'

Sarah's shoulders slumped, and she rubbed her eyes. 'Ask him. Let me know what he says.'

'Ok. I'll be in touch. Should I ring you back on this number?'

'No. I'll ring this afternoon.' She hung up and walked into the kitchen.

Ben turned to face her. 'You all right?'

'Yeah.' Wrapping her arms around Ben, she hugged him. 'Thanks for everything.'

'Hey, you.' Kissing the top of her head and hugging her back. 'I'd do it all again.'

June 26th 2012 – The police have charged Ben with assaulting Aaron. It's so unfair. He doesn't deserve this. Ben was only protecting me. Why should he suffer?

June 27th 2012 – I spoke to Aaron's solicitor and told him I'd be prepared to drop my complaint against him if Aaron dropped his allegation against Ben. I know it's not right he should get away with what he did to me. But seeing him get off scot-free is a small price to pay for keeping Ben out of court. Ben's given me everything. I know he would sacrifice himself for me. I can't let him do that. I've fallen for Ben Stainton. I tumbled headlong from a great height, and he caught me in his strong arms before I hit the ground. I dread to think where I would be without him.

Ben marched into the living room where Sarah sat reading. He stared at her. 'Why did you do it?' His face etched with sadness. 'He doesn't deserve to get away with what he did to you. He deserves to go to prison. At the very least, everyone should know what kind of man he is.'

Sarah lowered her eyes. 'He's rich and has powerful connections. He'd stop at nothing to see you in prison. I couldn't let that happen, after everything you've done for me.'

Ben ambled across to Sarah and sat beside her. He held her hand and squeezed. 'Are you sure you want to do this?'

She placed a finger to his lips. 'If it means keeping you here.'

He brushed the hair from her eyes, and edging nearer, moved his lips close to hers unsure if this is what she wanted. Sarah closed the gap between their mouths and kissed him.

June 28th, 2012 – *I thought Ben would be mad at what I did. He wasn't. We kissed and made love. I feel as if I've won the lottery of life. I don't have words to express how much I love him. He is … my universe.*

CHAPTER FOURTEEN

SEPTEMBER 2012 – Sarah had thought a lot about it. Her mind drifting back through time to her parents. Many years had elapsed since they had seen each other, more than a decade, her parting an acrimonious one. Back then she hated them. Loathed and detested their strictness. But the years which passed had not only brought about a longing but also wisdom. She now saw with blinding-clarity that her mum and dad just wanted the best for her. An only child. Gifts hadn't exactly been lavished on her, but she had enjoyed a happy childhood filled with pleasant memories. She now recognised, although she hadn't then, she was lucky, extremely lucky. After one massive argument with them, and full of anger, she had vowed to leave home. Having been befriended by another girl, Amanda, the pair hatched a plan.

Amanda hadn't enjoyed anything approaching a happy childhood. Hers had been in total contrast to Sarah's. Her father upped and left when she was small. Her mother and the string of men she introduced to Amanda, cared little about her welfare. It was a mystery to Sarah that Amanda remained so grounded and level-headed. Sarah wondered why her past self, having these two polar-opposite upbringings thrust before her, wasn't more grateful for her life. But a lot of what she did back then defied logic. Full of bravado the pair set off for the bright lights of London. Needless to say, the pavements were neither paved with gold or friendly faces as realisation soon dawned on the two of them. Only managing to find modestly-paid jobs, and unable to afford the high rent, they moved into a dingy house with two others, Chris and Gemma.

At first, the bohemian lifestyle they enjoyed seemed exciting, but gradually as drugs replaced alcohol as the substance of choice, their lives, her life, spiralled. After losing her job, her boss sick of her lateness and days off, it worsened. Stripped of the need to maintain a semblance of order in her life, she fell headlong into temptation. Weeks and months passed by, none of it very clear in Sarah's memory. Only a vague recollection of what occurred. She may have carried on this way, on her journey towards oblivion, but strung out and in need of a fix she entered Amanda's room. Her friend's lifeless body lay cold on the floor.

The weeks and months which followed still gave her nightmares. The faces of men she'd do a favour for, to procure her next high, taunted her. But above all this the sight of Amanda, stripped of life, haunted waking and sleeping hours. Something stirred in Sarah. In desperation and sheer strength of will, something she never knew existed in her, she sought help from a charity and slowly began to rebuild her life. The following months were hard, and to this day she was unsure how she managed to emerge from her tunnel of darkness.

She obtained a better job than her previous one and moved into a modest bedsit. She made friends and on an evening out, met Aaron. They clicked instantly. He swept her up in his high-powered life and convinced her to move North with him. In truth, she needed little persuasion. London was tainted with awful memories which brought a sour, sickly taste to her mouth.

She had considered contacting her parents on lots of occasions, but the embarrassment she felt about her time away prevented her from doing so. And as the months and years went by it became more difficult. The passing of time building a wall, brick by brick between the present and the past.

She discussed her childhood with Ben. Told him almost everything, leaving out the more shameful episodes. She couldn't admit them to herself never mind to the man she adored. He had been wonderful. Non-judgemental and sympathetic as he always was. He persuaded her to travel up to see her mother and father. *"You can't alter the past,"* he said. *"But you can write the future."* She felt scared, unsure as to how her arrival would be received. Were they even alive? If they were, would they hate her? She kept this to herself though, and didn't tell Ben. Did she truly want to go back there? She was unsure. But her childhood-past, her childhood home acted like the brightest of flames. Moth-like and unable to resist the pull, she went along with Ben's suggestion.

Ben drove along the avenue, dappled sunshine pushing its way through the tops of the tree-lined pavements. Sarah placed a hand on his and sighed as he pulled up.

He looked across at her. 'Everything ok?'

'I'm nervous that's all. It's been such a long time.'

'We don't have to do this. We can turn around, go home if you want.'

'We've travelled all this way though.'

Ben lifted a hand and placed it on her cheek. 'It doesn't matter. We'll go. Try again when you're more certain it's what you want.'

Sarah gazed to her left and along the road. Her stare resting on a middle-aged man mowing the lawn in one of the gardens.

Ben followed her gaze. 'Do you know him?'

She turned to face Ben. 'That's my dad.' Tears which had formed in her eyes slowly tumbled downwards. Ben pulled her close.

'You knew it would be hard.' Her sobbing relentless.

'I know.'

Her crying finally subsided, and Ben squeezed her hand. 'Shall we go? Or we could do this another day when—'

'No. I think I'm ready.'

'I'll be there with you. Things are never as bad as you think.'

Sarah forced a smile and got out. Ben clasped hold of her hand. The couple with measured steps crossed the road and strolled along the pavement. The man mowing paused and removed the grass box from the mower.

'Hello, Dad,' Sarah said.

The man spun on his heels and stared at her. His face breaking into a smile. 'Hello, Sarah.' He placed the grass box on the lawn and striding forward grasped her in his arms. She held on tight, relinquishing her grip reluctantly. 'I knew you'd come back one day,' he said.

'Where's Mum?' Sarah managed through tears.

'Alice,' shouted her dad. 'Alice, come out here.'

A woman appeared at the threshold. 'What's all the shouting …' her eyes met Sarah's, a hand involuntarily coming up to her mouth.

Sarah wandered forward. 'Hello, Mum.' The pair paused briefly before falling into each other's arms.

Ben and Sarah sat together on the settee as Sarah's mother and father came in from the kitchen with tea and biscuits.

'We'd better do introductions,' her dad said.

Sarah gazed at Ben and smiled. Ben gently squeezing her hand. 'This is Ben. My partner.'

Sarah's father stepped forward and shook Ben's hand. 'George. Nice to meet you, Ben. This is Alice.' Placing his arm around his wife.

Ben rose and shook hands with Sarah's mum. 'Alice,' he said. 'It's a pleasure to meet you.'

They talked and talked. Not of where Sarah had been all these years, but of childhood times. The albums and photos from her past happily displayed to Ben. And as he glanced through time towards her past, she watched him, smiling, trying to decipher his thoughts. Her eyes a study in concentration. Stories unfolded late into the evening. Finally Ben and Sarah stood to leave. Hugs were exchanged and kisses given. Promises made to visit each other.

As Ben and Sarah left in their car, her mother and father waved from the step of the house. Sarah continued to watch until they disappeared from view.

'I love you, Ben Stainton,' Sarah said. 'I didn't think I could love you any more than I did. But I love you more today.'

Ben smiled. 'I told you it wouldn't be so bad. You're their daughter. You never stop loving your kids.'

'I couldn't have done this without you.'

Ben tapped her hand. 'I was happy to come.'

'All those wasted years. I was a real handful.' Her eyes dropped to the floor. 'I thought maybe …'

'The past is gone. All you can do, all we can do, is write the future.'

'Thanks.'

'We don't need to go straight back. Your mam and dad were keen for us to stay.'

'I know. It's just … It may be too soon.'

'We could book into a hotel. Spend more time with them. Go back home tomorrow.'

Sarah smiled. 'Could we?'

'Yeah.'

Sarah frowned. 'What about clothes?'

'I packed some stuff. I thought this might happen.'

Sarah smiled and squeezed his hand. 'I love you a little bit more.'

'Of course you do,' he said.

September 2012 – *I told Ben, for the first time this morning I loved him. I thought it would be so hard. More difficult than writing it in my journal. But feelings are irrepressible. Sooner or later, they morph into words.*

CHAPTER FIFTEEN

JANUARY 2013 – Ben came bounding into the hall, glancing around as he raced through the lounge into the kitchen. 'You haven't seen my toolbox have you? The one with my good chisels?'

'Under the stairs,' Sarah said. 'I put it there last night after I nearly broke my leg on it.'

'Sorry sweetie.' Pulling his wife into his arms, he kissed her.

'You're forgiven.' She smiled and returned his kiss.

Ben glanced at the clock. 'If I wasn't late …'

Sarah huffed playfully. 'A wardrobe more important is it?'

Ben kissed her on the cheek and turned. 'Of course not, but I do need to see the owner before she leaves for work.'

'Ben?'

He stopped at the threshold. 'Yeah?'

'My period's late.'

Ben strode back across to her. 'Are you …'

'I haven't done a test or anything, but I'm usually pretty regular. If I was—'

'That'd be fantastic.' He placed a hand on either one of her arms. 'Are you sure?'

He kissed her again. 'Absolutely. You?'

She smiled 'Yes. I was worried … It's only six months since … I …'

'Six months, six years. What's the difference? I wouldn't love you any more than I do now.'

Sarah beamed. 'I love you, Ben.'

'Of course you do. I can put shelves up.'

'I'll do a pregnancy test.' Placing her hand on his cheek. 'And let you know.'

'Ring me.' Kissing her again, and then he was gone.

Sarah put a hand on her stomach and closed her eyes.

January 20th, 2013 – A day of ups and downs. My period was late. Ben was happy. I didn't know how he would react. I've done the test, but it was negative. By late afternoon the familiar dull-ache started in my belly. Just a false alarm. Ben was supportive. He told me we could try for real, now we both know for sure we want a baby.

January 21st, 2013 – Ben and I went out for a meal tonight. I thought it strange him taking me out on a Wednesday. Then I had the surprise of my life when he got down on one knee and proposed. I'm not even divorced from Aaron yet. I love this man. More and more each day. I accepted his proposal. Probably the easiest decision I'll ever have to make.

APRIL 2013 – Sarah ended the call and placed the handset back in its holder as Grace entered the shop.

Grace smiled and surveyed the room. 'I saw you open up. A new venture?'

'Only opened this week. A bit of a gamble I know, but I've always wanted to run a bookshop.'

'It's yours then?'

Sarah rolled her eyes. 'If you ignore the money we owe the bank. Anything in particular you're after?'

'Poetry,' Grace said.

'Modern or classical?'

'Classical.'

Sarah picked up the book Grace placed down on the counter. 'William Blake?' Sarah said.

Grace studied her. 'What do you think?'

'Bit too religious for my tastes. All that Jerusalem and that. There's one of his I quite like though. How—'

'How sweet I roamed?' Grace said.

Sarah smiled. 'Yes. It has a particular resonance for me. £9.99 please.'

Grace held her credit card up to the machine. The machine beeped signalling its approval. Sarah popped the book and receipt into a bag and handed it to Grace.

Grace smiled. 'Thanks.' And headed for the door.

She watched as Grace left and made her way to the rear of the shop. Ben was outside in the yard constructing a bookshelf.

She stood at the threshold near to him. 'Aaron's solicitor phoned.'

He stopped what he was doing and looked up. 'What did he say?' Tossing his saw on the bench.

'He's offered me £100,000. He says it's his final offer.'

'What are you going to do? You know I'll support you, whatever you decide.'

Sarah stepped forward and put her hand on his arm. 'What do you think?'

Ben pulled her closer. 'For what he put you through. You deserve it all.' Moving a hand to her cheek, he stared intensely into her eyes.

'I'll be able to give you back the money you loaned me for the shop. And it'll help to reduce the mortgage.'

'I don't want the money back. That's my stake in this business. Pay off the mortgage in full, and I'll be a sleeping partner. Besides, we'll be getting married soon.'

'Are you sure you want to marry me?'

He kissed her on the cheek. 'Never more so. If it doesn't work out, I'll have all the detective novels.'

Sarah smiled briefly. She lowered her head a little. 'It would bring an end to it. The divorce will soon be finalised, and it means I … we, can move on.'

'Sarah,' he said. Pulling her into him. 'If you're happy. So am I.'

September 16th, 2013 – *I've decided to accept Aaron's terms. I could push for more, but I'm exhausted by it all. Although we're getting divorced, the wound will never heal fully until I remove him from my life for good. Ben was so supportive, but then he always is. My towering piece of granite.*

October 19th, 2013 – *Another month, another period. I worry that what Aaron did has damaged me somehow. What if I can't get pregnant? I daren't tell Ben about my concerns. I want to, but I can't. Not yet.*

CHAPTER SIXTEEN

MARCH 2014 – Ben and Sarah's wedding morning was a sunny affair. The poor weather from the week before giving way to bright, spring-like warmth. Sarah sat at her dressing table as a woman applied her make-up.

Mary entered the bedroom and perched on the edge of the bed. 'I've just got off the phone with Toby. Ben's fine. He didn't get too drunk last night.'

Sarah sighed. 'Good. I had visions of him being blotto at the service. I told him to have his stag-night on Thursday.'

'You know Ben. Or should I say some of his mates from the Rugby club.'

'Mum and Dad ok?' Sarah said.

'You mum's fine. Your dad seems nervous though. He's going over his speech again.'

'He'll be fine,' Sarah said.

The woman applying the make-up stepped back. 'What do you think?' she said.

Sarah smiled. 'It's fantastic.' Turning to face Mary.

Mary beamed. 'You're gorgeous. Ben will be blown away.'

Ben, carrying his jacket, stepped through the door into the living room. Toby and Stan both seated, looked towards him.

Stan glanced at the clock. 'We wondered if you were ever coming.'

Toby chuckled. 'We thought you'd chickened out.'

Ben threw his jacket over the back of the settee. 'I wanted to look my best for Sarah. What do you think?' Straightening his tie, he checked his appearance in the mirror.

Stan stood and patted his friend on the arm. 'You'll do.' Grinning at him.

Toby got to his feet, picked up Ben's jacket and tossed it to him. 'Get this on. The cars waiting.'

Ben glanced at his watch. 'Already?'

Toby rolled his eyes. 'It's the bride's prerogative to be late. Not the grooms.'

Ben pulled on his jacket. 'Lead on,' he said.

Stan tugged his arm. 'Aren't you forgetting something.' Holding out his hand.

Ben lowered his eyes. 'What?'

'The ring,' Toby said.

Ben slapped his head. 'Of course.' Bounding from the room and up the stairs.

Toby nudged Stan. 'Speech all done?'

Stan patted his pocket. 'Oh yes.'

'Would you like me to give it a read through for you? I've been best man a number of times.'

Stan smiled. 'Thanks. But you'll have to wait like the rest of them.'

Toby winked. 'Worth a try. I have a few funny stories about Ben I could tell you.'

Stan smiled. 'Thanks, Toby, but I've got all the material I need.'

Sarah's mum and dad stood in the front room of Mary's house as Sarah entered. Her dad, his eyes glued to his speech barely looked up.

Sarah's mum's hand shot to her mouth as she caught sight of her daughter. Tears glistened in her eyes. 'Oh, Sarah.' Walking across and hugging her daughter. 'You look wonderful.'

Her dad smiled broadly. 'Wow,' he said. 'You'll knock them dead.'

Mary entered accompanied by a man carrying a camera.

'Bride and Father of the Bride,' he said.

Sarah focussed on the photographer. 'Yes please.'

Ben blew his cheeks out and looked at Stan. 'I'm getting a little nervous. I wish I'd had a drink now.'

Stan nudged him. 'You don't want to turn up for your wedding stinking of booze. You'll be fine.'

The vicar appeared from a side door and stopped at the front of the altar. He motioned for the congregation to stand as the music resounded. Ben and Stan stepped forward facing the front. Ben sneaked a peek over his shoulder as Sarah, accompanied by her father, slowly walked forward.

Ben hoisted Sarah up into his arms and pushed open the door with the side of his knee, carrying her inside. Kissing her passionately then placing her gently on the floor.

'Home, Mrs Stainton,' he said.

'I'll never get tired of hearing you say that.' She stretched up and kissed him.

'Nightcap?' he said.

'I've had enough. I'm knackered.'

Ben nodded, taking hold of his wife's hand. 'Me too. It's amazing how tiring getting married is.'

Sarah smiled and winked at him. 'Maybe we should go to bed.'

'Do you think so?' Pulling her close, he comically lowered his eyes.

'A marriage isn't legal until it's consummated.'

Ben lifted her up in his arms again. 'Ok. Let's seal this deal.'

'Ben,' she said. 'I love you so much. I couldn't be happier.'

He continued up the stairs. 'Me too. I feel incredibly lucky.'

They reached the top and Ben pushed open the bedroom door, continuing inside. Placing his wife on the bed, he reached into his trouser pocket and pulled out a small jewellery box. 'I got you this.' Handing Sarah the box.

Inside a gold chain with two doves hanging from it. She smiled, leant forward and kissed him.

CHAPTER SEVENTEEN

APRIL 2014 – Ben came striding into the shop from the back, placing a box on the counter. 'That's the last of the books.'

'Have you time for a coffee?' Sarah said.

'I'm in a bit of a rush.' Kissing her on the cheek. 'Why?'

'I was thinking of joining a class.'

'Class?' Collecting his jacket from behind the counter. 'What kind?'

'Creative writing.'

'Well, you've got lots of inspiration.' Scanning the shop, he pointed around.

She nodded. 'I thought it might take my mind off the hospital appointment.'

Ben walked back across to her, pulling her close. 'It'll be okay. Don't go worrying about that. This time next year we'll have a little baby on the way. You just watch.'

'Have I told you how much I love you, Ben Stainton?' She kissed him.

'Loads, Mrs Stainton.'

'Go on. Off you go. I'll see you tonight. Don't forget the wine though.'

'I won't.'

'Thanks, gorgeous.'

Sarah studied the flyer, and re-read the words. She picked up the phone and dialled a number.

'Teesside University enrolment?' a female voice said.

'I'll like to enrol on the creative writing course please.'

'Of course. I just need a few details.'

Ben and Sarah approached the house, and Ben knocked on the door. It swung open. Toby stood inside holding a glass of wine.

'Ben, Sarah.' Shaking his brother-in-law's hand and kissing Sarah warmly. 'Come in.'

They followed Toby inside, making their way through the throng of people, into the dining room.

Mary threw her arms around Ben, kissing him on the cheek. 'Bennie-boy. How is he measuring up, Sarah? Now you're married.' Embracing Sarah and kissing her sister-in-law on both cheeks.

Sarah took hold of Ben's hand. 'He's wonderful. I'm fortunate.'

Mary grasped hold of Sarah's other hand. 'Come over here you two. There are some people I'd like you to meet.'

Sarah sat on the settee as Mary flopped onto the seat next to her. Ben, in conversation with Toby—on the other side of the room—occasionally glanced towards Sarah, who smiled back at him.

'You ok, Sarah?' Mary asked. 'You look a little down.'

Sarah forced a smile. 'I'm all right.'

Mary gently squeezed Sarah's hand. 'It will happen. Give it time.'

'What if I can't.' Turning her head to face Mary, she frowned.

'It hasn't been long. It took Toby and I ages. You can't rush nature.'

Sarah dropped her eyes down. 'I know. We have an appointment next week. At the fertility clinic.'

'Well, that's good. Isn't it?'

'I suppose. What if ...'

Ben, excused himself and joined them. 'What are you two plotting?'

Mary smiled. 'Nothing. Women's talk, that's all.'

April 2014 – We went to Mary and Toby's. It was their wedding anniversary. I chatted with Mary about my concerns over not getting pregnant. She tried to allay my fears. If only life was so simple. I love words. Their power, their potency. But even words, with all their majesty, are impotent in the face of fear.

I long for you, my lost beguile
To touch your face and see your smile
And hold you close in warm embrace
To then understand the grace
And truly know that we are whole
To feel the throb within my soul
To hear your warmth in playful cries
And view our past, through timeless eyes
I long to hold your childish hand
And see his face on virgin land
rise within my captured view
I long for you, I long for you.

CHAPTER EIGHTEEN

MAY 2014 - Sarah and Ben sat quietly in the consultation room. Ben holding on tightly to his wife's hand, gently squeezed it as Sarah forced a smile.

The door opened, and a woman carrying a folder strode in. She positioned herself behind her desk and smiled at the pair. 'How are you two?'

Ben glanced at his wife. 'Good.'

The woman opened the folder and viewed the documents inside. 'We have the results back, and it's good news.'

Ben and Sarah beamed.

The woman flicked through the pages and stopped. 'There's nothing physically wrong with either of you—'

Sarah leant forward. 'I was worried that.' She paused and glanced at Ben. 'I may be damaged in some way.'

The woman eyed Sarah. 'Damaged?'

Ben patted his wife's hand. 'What Sarah means, Doctor.' Smiling at his wife. 'She was in an accident a while back, and she was afraid it might have affected her chances of conceiving.'

The doctor clasped her hands together. 'There's nothing physically wrong with you, Sarah.'

'Why haven't I got pregnant then?'

'Mother nature's funny. Sometimes she won't be rushed. What I tell my patients, patients like yourself, is to relax. Take a holiday. Let nature take its course.'

'It's been over a year,' Sarah said.

'That's not a long time. I've got a couple of brochures here.' Pulling them from her folder, she placed them down. 'It gives information on what to do to give yourself the best chance of conceiving.'

Sarah lowered her eyes. 'What if …'

The doctor smiled again. 'Let's cross that bridge if we reach it. Give it a while longer and see what happens. If you still haven't conceived, we'll consider our options.'

Sarah leant forward, and Ben patted her knee. 'What options would we have?' Ben said.

'Well.' Glancing at her file. 'We can prescribe medication to increase the likelihood—'

'Why can't you give me something now?' Sarah said.

Ben patted his wife's knee again and fixed his attention back on the Doctor. 'I'm forty-two, Doctor.'

'I know, Ben. I understand your frustration. I could tell you about countless couples in your situation. Give it time.' She leant back in her chair and tapped her lips with a finger. 'We'll make an appointment for three months time. If nothing's happened, we'll see what we can do.'

Ben smiled at his wife who smiled back.

'Book an appointment with my secretary on your way out. But don't worry. It will happen.'

Ben and Sarah stood. Ben offering his hand. 'Thanks, Doctor.'

She shook his and then Sarah's. 'I'll see you soon. If you fall pregnant in the meantime, let us know.'

Sarah nodded at her, and taking hold of Ben's hand they left.

Ben flopped into the driver's seat and looked across at his wife. 'It was good news.'

She squeezed his hand. 'I love you, Ben. I'm so happy, and I know I shouldn't want more, but—'

He put a hand on her cheek and gently kissed her. 'Shall we go home and make babies?'

Sarah nodded, and Ben started the van. He glanced at her. 'Mary asked if we wanted to come to the villa with her and Toby. I thought with what the doctor said …'

'I'd like that. But what about the shop?'

'We'll get someone to look after it. We can book to go on our own if you'd rather?'

Sarah shook her head. 'I like Mary and Toby. I'd love to go with them.'

'I'll ring Mary later. An old school friend of a mine has a daughter who's at University. She's searching for work. Maybe you could train her up?'

'Have you been plotting this, Ben?'

He winked at his wife. 'No. We deserve a break. And well …'

Sarah patted his hand. 'Thanks.'

'For what?'

'For everything.'

Ben smiled and kissed his wife.

JUNE 2014 - Ben ambled across to the pool and stopped, putting his arms around his wife. Sarah jumped. Moving back from the edge.

'Come on in Sarah,' shouted one of the boys.

'Is it cold?' she said.

'No,' shouted the boys in unison.

Ben put his mouth to Sarah's ear. 'Do you want to go in?'

'Don't you dare push me, Ben Stainton.' she said.

'Who said I was going to push you?' Hoisting his wife into his arms.

'Ben Stainton put me down this instant.'

He walked to the edge and stopped. 'A kiss and I may give you reprieve.'

She smiled. Closing her eyes, she dramatically looked away. 'I don't respond to blackmail.'

He held her out in his massive arms. 'Are you sure?'

'You're a brute.' She grinned. 'Terrifying a young woman like this.'

He pulled her back into his arms and kissed her. The two boys stared at each other and pulled faces. 'Throw her, throw her,' they chanted.

Sarah laughed and then pouted at him. 'Ben. Don't you dare.'

He gently tossed his wife towards the pool and watched as she splashed into the water. The two boys clambering across to her, laughing.

'Sorry,' he said. 'I lost my grip.'

Sarah stood in the water with her hands on her hips. Bedraggled hair half covering her face. 'I'll get you back for this.' She shook her fist in a mock gesture. Ben blew her a kiss and turned walking back to his sunbed.

Sarah turned and looked at the two boys. Pushing the hair over her head. 'Who wants a race?'

'We do,' they said.

Ben slumped next to Mary who looked up from her magazine. 'You're a big kid, you.'

He turned and fixed her with a stare. 'There's room in the pool for another.' Lowering his eyes, he wagged his finger.

Mary flicked a page across her magazine. 'You've never been brave enough, Bennie-boy.'

'Where's Toby?' he said.

'He's gone to hire a car. We're taking the boys to the water park. You and Sarah are welcome to come.'

'I think we'll just chill a little.'

Mary nodded towards Sarah. 'Any news on the …'

'Nothing yet. That's why we've come away. The Doctor said it may help us having a break.'

Mary put a hand on his arm. ' It's probably the best thing to do. It will happen. You just have to be patient.'

He half-smiled at his sister. 'You know I've always wanted kids. But I'd sort of accepted I would never be a dad. Being an uncle to your two rascals is enough, but—'

Mary put aside her magazine, and turned so that she was facing her brother. 'But?'

'Sarah wants one so bad. I feel for her every month when nothing happens. She doesn't say, but it's crushing her.'

'What did the hospital tell you?'

'We checked out fine medically. They told us to leave it for three months, and if Sarah hasn't fallen they'll try something else.'

'There you are. You're worrying about nothing.'

'Your friend? The one who had IVF.'

'Tina?' Mary said.

'Yeah. How did they go about it?'

'Ben. It's still early. Tina and Jake tried for four years.'

Ben forced a smile. 'But it's an option.'

'Her first two attempts failed. They paid for more treatments. It—'

Ben stared into Mary's eyes. 'I'm not bothered how much money it costs.' Glancing towards Sarah splashing around with the boys. 'You can't put a price on happiness.'

Mary lifted a hand to his cheek and smiled. 'No you can't.'

Mary linked Sarah's arm. 'Come on. Let's go and do some shopping.'

'What about Ben, Toby and the boys?' Sarah said. 'Aren't they coming?'

Mary tutted. 'They're playing football. Toby and Ben still believe they're teenagers. They'll come back limping with aches and pains. Luckily, I've some painkillers in here.' Patting her handbag, she grinned.

'I thought I might buy Ben something.'

'Clothes?'

Sarah shook her head. 'A watch. The one he wears is always losing time.'

Mary laughed. 'I know. It was dad's.'

'Oh. I didn't know.'

'Ben and Dad were extremely close. He worked with him from being a kid. He can't bear to part with anything that belonged to Dad. All his tools and DIY manuals.'

Sarah frowned. 'Maybe a watch is not a good idea then?'

'Don't be daft. If you buy it for him, he'll wear it. He loves you.'

'But if he treasures his Dad's—'

'If you want to put up with Ben's tardiness your entire married life, don't get a new one.' She held out her hands. 'But if you'd like a reasonably punctual husband …'

Sarah smiled. 'I know what you mean. Ok. Let's do it.'

They strolled on further. Sarah stopped outside a boutique with children's clothes on display in the window. Mary took hold of her hand squeezing it gently. 'It will happen, Sarah. Give it time.'

'I know. It's just … I know how much Ben wants children. I've seen the way he dotes on your two. He would make such a wonderful dad.' She turned to face Mary. 'I want so much to make him happy. Ben's everything to me.'

Mary put a hand on her cheek. 'You two.' Her eyes reddening slightly. 'What are you like?'

'What do you mean?'

'Nothing. You're incredibly lucky to have one another.'

Sarah smiled. 'I know. I know.'

OCTOBER 2014 – Sarah perched on the edge of the bed staring down at the wrapping from her tampon. She placed a hand on her stomach, the ache she felt there nothing compared to the one in her heart. She closed her eyes and willed the tears collecting there to remain. A sadness crept through her. A longing for something. Someone who didn't even exist. She stood and marched across to the wardrobe, dropping onto her knees she searched for the diary. Finding it, she rocked back on her haunches and read. The words from her time with Aaron washing over her. Sarah smiled to herself and slammed the book shut. How stupid she was. Look what she had in her life now. Ben and his love. This house. No longer confined in a violent, loveless marriage.

'You're stupid,' she whispered.

If she never got pregnant so what? She had happiness. She had Ben. She had her shop and all the other things which made her life a joy now. Be thankful for what you have. Sarah wiped her eyes with the sleeve of her dressing gown as footsteps sounded from outside the bedroom. She hastily deposited her journal into her handbag and tossed it on the bed as Ben entered.

'Morning gorgeous.' He kissed his wife.

'Morning,' she said.

'What have you got planned for today?'

Sarah glanced across at her handbag. 'I'm meeting a friend for a coffee. You?'

'Mary needs a job doing. I'm off across there now.'

Sarah kissed him. 'I'll have a quick shower, and you can drop me off if you like.'

'Yeah, no problem.'

Sarah headed into the en-suite. Ben peered at the tampon packaging on the bed and then towards the bathroom his wife had entered. He frowned, shook his head and left.

Sarah bounded down the stairs and into the living room. Ben stood waiting as she entered. He strode across and hugged her, tightly.

'What was that for?' Looking up at him, she smiled.

'Because I love you and always will. No matter what.'

Sarah paused before allowing her lips to meet his.

CHAPTER NINETEEN

Emily stopped at a stand just inside the restaurant. The sign pinned to it informing customers to *wait to be seated*, at the entrance to the restaurant. A member of staff hurried across. Immaculately dressed, he smiled at her.

'I'm meeting a friend of mine,' Emily said. 'He's booked a table in my name. Emily Kirkby.'

The man perused the list in front of him. 'If you'd follow me.'

The pair of them snaked their way through the room passing other diners en route. Finally, they stopped at one where Emily sat.

He handed her a menu. 'Can I get you a drink?'

'A glass of Merlot please.'

He smiled, nodded politely and left. Emily sat back and waited for Oliver's arrival. Her meetings with him had increased in regularity as she completed more of the book. She glanced at her watch. He was seldom on time. She had become accustomed to this particular facet of his personality. Emily pulled out her mobile and checked for messages. There weren't any. She was contemplating phoning Lisa when she sighted Oliver scanning the room.

He spotted her and hurried across slumping in the seat opposite. 'Sorry I'm late.'

Emily tutted and raised her eyes upward. 'You're always late.'

He smiled. 'I do have other clients, Emily.'

She shook her head and squeezed her eyes shut. 'Sorry, Oliver. I'm tired.'

'Have you ordered?'

'Only a drink for me … I wasn't sure what you wanted.'

The waiter arrived back placing a glass in front of her. He focused on Oliver. 'Can I get you a drink, sir?'

'Large brandy with ice,' Oliver said.

'Would you like a few more moments to decide.' Glancing at the menu Oliver held.

Oliver glanced up. 'I'll have the salmon.'

Emily handed her menu to the waiter. 'A green salad please.'

He jotted down their order and left.

He fixed Emily with a stare. 'You ok?'

She brought her hands up to her face and sighed. 'Like I said, I'm tired. I haven't been sleeping well.'

'You and Richard?'

She shrugged. 'I'm sure you didn't ask me here to speak about Richard and me?'

Oliver widened his eyes. 'No. But I'm more than just your agent. I thought we were friends?'

Emily lowered her head. 'I'm sorry. I'm not very good company tonight.'

He placed a hand on hers. 'Anything I can help with?'

'Just life. Sometimes it gets you down. I'll be all right tomorrow.'

Oliver nodded. 'If you need to talk …?'

Emily forced a smile. 'I know. Thanks.'

'Well.' He said. Clasping his hands together, he sat back in his seat. 'How's the writing going?'

Emily reached into her bag and pulled out a file pushing it across the table towards him. 'Ok. I've managed another five chapters.'

He grinned. 'You can make the deadline then?'

She nodded. 'I'll make it.'

'Good. I knew you would.'

I met Oliver tonight. I was terrible company. I didn't feel like going out at all. I would have prefered a glass of wine and an early night if I'm honest. It's the moments alone in a public place when I have the most troubling thoughts. Strange, when I'm at home it's different. They never seem to arrive, my flat acting like a defensive shield. I glimpsed a word on the front of a broadsheet a man was reading at a nearby table. *Tragedy.* I vividly remember reading it. I couldn't make out the story it was too far away. But it wouldn't have mattered. Tragedy is everywhere if you care to look. It lives around and within us. It passes us by on a busy street, or sits on a bench in the park. Tragedy is an empty cot, or a simple gold band which once adorned a finger. A tattered photograph, or a pair of long-forgotten shoes. It's where love and hope go to die. It is relentless and pursues us all, striking when we least expect it. With no shape or form, sound or odour, it arrives unwanted and unexpected like an uninvited guest. Sometimes, however, the seed of tragedy is sown long before it appears. Sometimes tragedy begins as something insignificant. Something so trivial, we can miss it altogether. Sometimes tragedy wears the coat of innocence. As simple as someone sat in a coffee shop, stirring their skinny latte.

Sarah waved at Grace across the café, and made a drinking gesture with her hand. Grace, understanding, lifted her half-full cup and shook her head, mouthing a no thank you. Sarah got served and joined her friend.

'How was the holiday?' Grace said.

'Great. We had a wonderful time.'

'Manage any writing?'

'A little. You lose yourself in the sun and sangria though. What have you been up to?'

'Not a lot. Ricky and I had a couple of days away though. Nothing exotic. York.'

Sarah smiled. 'I love York. Such an atmospheric place.'

'Yeah. The weather was wonderful too. I have a nice task for the writing group.'

'Do I get a heads up?'

Grace smiled. 'Favouritism? That would never do, would it?'

Sarah put a hand on her stomach. 'I don't suppose so.'

'You all right?' Grace said.

Sarah frowned. 'My period.'

'The curse women have to live with. Do you suffer bad pains?'

Sarah shook her head. 'Not really it's just …' She paused. 'Ben and I are trying for a baby. Every passing month … it's stupid I know … but we …' She reached into her handbag and plucked a tissue from it.

Grace held her hand. 'It's not stupid. Have you tried for very long?'

'Seems like a lifetime. Over a year.'

'That's not a long—'

'Everyone says that, Grace. It's just when you want something so bad, and it doesn't happen, you die a little each month. I want it more for Ben. He'd loves kids.'

Grace felt guilt course through her. The memory of the abortion she'd had, some time ago, pushed hard for her attention.

Sarah blew her nose. 'Have you ever wanted children?'

Grace shifted in her seat. 'Not really. I had my job. It's something that's never come up.'

'What would you do if you fell—'

'Unlikely. I'm on the pill. I make Ricky wear a condom as well. I haven't known him long … and well … I don't want to take chances. So If I did fall pregnant, I'd call it Houdini.'

Sarah laughed. 'Yeah.'

Grace put a hand on hers. 'Give it some time. There are always alternatives like IVF.'

'Ben and I discussed it. We have an appointment at the fertility clinic soon. They said if I hadn't fallen within three months they'd consider giving us some help.'

Grace smiled. 'There you are. They'll get you pregnant. I'm sure.'

Sarah opened her bag and glimpsed inside. Satisfied, she picked it up and stood. 'I'm nipping to the toilet.' As she turned she collided with a waiter carrying cups and saucers. The clatter and smash of china and pottery resounded around the room. Sarah was sent sprawling forward. Her handbag knocked from her hand, flying across the floor, scattering the contents about.

Grace stood and helped her to her feet. 'Are you ok?' Leading her back to her seat.

The waiter turned, profusely mouthing apologies to her. 'It's fine,' she said. 'I'm not hurt.'

Grace picked up the bag and assisted by a female customer, retrieved the contents. Handing the bag to Sarah. Sarah blushed. The sight of her tampons on the floor filling her with embarrassment.

'Are you sure you're ok?' Grace asked.

Sarah stood. 'Fine, fine. I'll be back in a minute.' Racing towards the toilets, she shot inside the door.

Grace sat, as the waiter swept up the debris.

He stooped and plucked something up from under the table. 'Is this your friend's?' he said.

Grace accepted the diary from him. 'Yes, I think so.' Putting the book on the table, she glanced at it. The waiter tidied up the final remnants and disappeared behind the counter.

Grace looked back at the book, her interest piqued. She picked it up and read. Quickly flicking through the pages. The words so vivid, they jumped out at her. She peered across to the other side of the room as Sarah came out, and dropped the book into her handbag. Sarah motioned at her and nodded towards the door. Grace took the hint and followed her friend outside.

Grace caught her up. 'What's up, Sarah?'

'God. I've never felt so embarrassed. My tampons all over the floor.'

Grace took hold of Sarah's arm. 'I don't think anyone noticed. They were probably busy on their mobile's.'

'Of course they did. Those young lads on the next table couldn't keep a straight face.'

Grace giggled. 'I'm sorry.'

Sarah laughed. 'It's not funny, Grace.' The pair collapsing in hysterics.

'Forget about it,' Grace said. 'Let's go and do a bit of shopping.'

Sarah rolled her eyes and shook her head. 'It'll be a long time before I forget about this.'

Grace waved Sarah off as she inserted her key and entered her flat. She eased off her coat and draped it on the bannister newel-post. After making herself a cup of tea, she slumped onto a seat in the dining room. Opening her bag, and retrieving her phone, she spotted Sarah's diary inside. Plucking it from her handbag she paused. She shouldn't be reading it. It was Sarah's, after all. Tentatively she opened it up. It was an old one. Going back to 2012. Why was she carrying around an old diary? She turned the first page and began to read.

Sarah emptied her handbag onto the bed. She frantically searched through the contents. It wasn't there. She was sure she had it the other day. She pondered for a moment, and moving across to the wardrobe opened a drawer and pulled out the journals. Rifling through them she tossed them into the drawer. Sarah brought her hands to her face, desperately trying to remember when she had last seen it. Racing downstairs she checked drawers and cupboards. Under the settee and seats. Behind and beneath cupboards. Maybe Ben had found it she wondered. Snatching her mobile with shaking hands, she phoned.

'Hi, gorgeous,' he said.

'Hi. You didn't come across a book of mine did you?'

'Book? What sort of book?'

'One of my old journals.'

'No, why?'

'Nothing really. I must have put it down somewhere. Don't worry.'

'Are you ok?' he said.

'Fine. How's the job going?'

'I should be finished this week.'

'Good. I'll prepare something nice for tea, shall I?'

'Lovely. I'll be home about six,' he said.

'Yeah. I'll grab something on the way home from the shop. Love you.'

'Love you too. Are you sure everything's all right?' he said.

'I'm fine. Just a little tired. See you later, handsome.'

Sarah hung up and glanced at the clock. Snatching her house and car keys, she rushed out.

Sarah entered the coffee shop and headed across to the counter. A young woman looked up from her phone and smiled. 'What can I get you?'

'A medium latte to go please.'

'Anything else?'

'No. That's all. Except … There hasn't been a diary handed in has there?'

'I can check in our lost property if you like.'

'Yes please,' Sarah said.

The woman dropped to her knees and picked up a box. Rifling through its contents, she held out a book. 'Is this it?'

Sarah's eyes widened peering over the counter. She frowned. 'No, that's not it.'

'It's the only one in here.'

'Ok,' Sarah said.

The woman finished making the drink and placed it on the counter in front of Sarah. '£2.60 please.'

Sarah paid for the drink and left. Walking the short distance to her shop, she stopped outside and took a deep breath. Tears welled in her eyes. She let out a long sigh, and opened the shutter.

CHAPTER TWENTY

DECEMBER 2015 - Sarah, holding tightly onto Ben stared towards the floor deep in thought.

Ben squeezed her hand and smiled at her. 'You ok?'

'It's such a lot of money, Ben. What happens if ...?'

He placed a hand on her cheek. 'Money doesn't matter. It's our, your happiness which does.'

She forced a smile. 'I know. Is it what you want though?'

'I want you to be happy. I'd do anything to make that happen. If we don't have children, it won't alter that.'

'I shouldn't want more. I'm so lucky to have found you ... when I think about the life I had with Aaron ...' She placed a hand over her mouth as a gasp escaped.

'Hey,' Ben said. 'That's in the past.'

She leant forward and kissed him on the cheek.

The consultation room door opened. A woman doctor walked in, smiled at the pair, and sat opposite them. 'How are you two?'

Ben glanced at Sarah. 'We're fine, Doctor.'

'Good, good. Right.' Opening the file she held, she flicked through the pages. 'Today I'm going to explain to you.' She glanced between the couple. 'What's involved in IVF. If you have any questions just ask. Ok?'

The pair nodded.

She studied her notes. 'Was everything all right with the counselling?'

Sarah nodded and looked at Ben who squeezed her hand again. 'It was very helpful,' she said.

'Good. Are there any questions you want to ask me?'

The pair shook their heads.

'Have you read the information sent out to you?'

Ben rubbed the stubble on his chin. 'We have.'

The doctor leant in closer. 'I'll run through it again. Just to make sure you understand it fully and you're happy with the procedure. Today you're going to receive some medication.' She clasped her hands together. 'This is given to stop your periods.' Looking across at Sarah who nodded. 'We do this to make the drugs given in the next stage more effective. This drug is administered by you.' She smiled at Sarah. 'Either by injection or nasal spray. How do you feel about that?'

'I'm fine with needles,' Sarah said. 'But I'd rather have the spray.'

The doctor nodded. 'That's fine.' And made a note in her file.

'How long do I take it for?' Sarah said.

'Two weeks.' Sarah nodded. 'After this, we give you a daily injection of a follicle-stimulating hormone. This is done for 10-12 days. I'm afraid you'll need to administer this yourself. Are you ok with that?'

Sarah glanced at Ben. 'Ben will help me with it.'

The doctor smiled at Ben. 'The clinic will monitor your ovaries via ultrasound scans. When we're happy, a final hormone injection is given. It helps to mature the eggs. This happens 34 to 38 hours before collection.' The doctor glanced between Sarah and her notes.

Sarah smiled at Ben. 'I understand.'

The doctor continued. 'On the day of your procedure, we'll sedate you. The eggs are then collected using a needle passed through the vagina and into the ovary.'

'How long will it take?' Sarah said.

'About twenty minutes.'

'Is it painful?'

'The procedure itself isn't, but it may result in cramping and bleeding.'

Sarah nodded. 'Ok.'

'Good.' Pulling out a piece of paper from her file she handed it to Sarah. 'There's information in here on how to prepare yourself on the day. The clinic will continue to provide counselling throughout the procedure.'

The couple nodded.

'Once we've collected the eggs, Ben.' Looking across at him. 'We'll need you to provide a sample of semen.'

'Looks like I have it easy,' Ben said.

The doctor smiled. 'You do. But it's a crucial role you play. We can't do it without you.'

Sarah lightly squeezed Ben's hand. 'You'll be my support.' He gently squeezed her back.

The doctor continued. 'The eggs and sperm are mixed together, and then checked after 16 to 20 hours to see if fertilisation has taken place.'

'If they haven't fertilised?' Sarah said.

'We repeat the process,' the doctor said. 'Don't worry though. The success rate is high. When we have the fertilised eggs, we grow them for six days. The best one or two embryos are chosen for transfer. We'll administer some more hormones to ready your womb.'

Sarah and Ben nodded again.

'A few days later the embryos are placed in the womb with a catheter. This is a simple process and doesn't require any sedation.'

'How many embryos are placed in my womb?'

'Because you're under thirty-seven, only one. Provided they are of good quality. If not we'll hedge our bets and put more in. Are you two ok with this?'

They nodded in unison. 'It's fine,' Sarah said.

The doctor leant forward in her chair. 'After this, a test will be carried out two weeks later to see if you're pregnant. This can be the most difficult time emotionally. This is where you can help, Ben.'

Ben gently squeezed his wife's hand. 'Of course.' Smiling at Sarah, reassuringly.

Sarah frowned. 'What happens if it's unsuccessful?'

'We generally ask the patient to wait two months before trying again.'

Sarah's eyes lowered. Ben studied her. 'Let's be positive,' he said. 'Bridges are for crossing when you reach them.'

'Very true,' the doctor said. 'Any questions?'

Sarah glanced at Ben and shook her head. Ben turned to face the doctor once more. 'I think you've covered everything,' he said.

The doctor stood. 'Good. I'll pop outside and send someone along to discuss the paperwork and organise a date for the procedure.'

'Thank you,' Sarah said. The doctor smiled politely and left.

'You ok with this?' Ben said.

'Yeah.' She reached across to Ben and kissed him. 'Thanks. For everything.'

Ben cupped her chin with his hand. 'I love you, Sarah. So much.'

DECEMBER 2015 – Visited the fertility clinic with Ben today. We decided to go private as the wait on the NHS was too long. It's costing us £5,000 for the first cycle of treatment. The whole process takes about two months, and my appointment is for late January. I hope and pray it's the only one I need. Ben is so supportive. But then he always is. I'm looking forward to Christmas. Mary and Toby have invited us over. We're going to visit my parents next week. I'm not bothered what I have under the tree this year, but next year I hope it's full of presents for our baby. The wanting, the desire for a child, is simultaneously exciting and crushing. I cling to hope. I cling to Ben.

CHAPTER TWENTY-ONE

JANUARY 2016 – Sarah lay in bed. Her headache had eased a little, but nausea clung to her.

Ben walked in carrying a glass of water and two tablets. 'How are you feeling?'

Sarah eased herself up. 'A little better. My headaches not as bad, but I still feel sick.'

'Take these.' Handing her the tablets and the water.

'I'm not sure I can keep them down.'

'Just try. For me.'

Sarah forced a smile. Popping the tablets into her mouth, she took a swig of liquid and handed Ben the glass back. 'Did you phone the clinic?'

'I did. They may have a cancellation next month. They're ringing back.'

'It's so frustrating, I—'

Ben placed a hand on Sarah's. 'Don't worry. It's only a short delay. Get yourself well.'

Sarah blinked. 'What about the shop?'

'I've got Annie looking after it for the next couple of days. She's not back at University until Wednesday. I've rearranged a few things as well, so we should be ok for the rest of the week.'

'Hopefully, I'll be better by next week.'

'Hopefully.' He kissed her on the head. 'Get some sleep, I'll check on you later.'

Sarah shuffled down in the bed and closed her eyes as Ben made his way out.

He paused at the threshold, looking back at his wife. 'It will happen,' he said.

Sarah raised her head a little. 'I know.'

He smiled and closed the door gently behind him.

Sarah closed her eyes and caressed the dove around her neck.

TWO WEEKS LATER – Sarah made her way out of the creative writing course and down the stairs. She paused at the bottom and opened her bag. Sighing she turned, bounded back up the stairs and into the classroom. Grace, who was positioned behind her desk looked up.

Sarah smiled back, and playfully slapped her forehead. She plucked a piece of paper lying on the table. 'I'll forget my head one day.' And held the paper aloft. 'The assignment you gave us.'

'You would struggle to write anything without it.'

'See you next week,' Sarah said.

'Sarah,' Grace said. Lowering her voice. 'Any news on the baby front.'

She turned around to face her. 'Not yet. That virus I had meant we had to cancel my appointment. We have a new one pencilled in for the end of next month.'

'Good. I'm sure it'll go well.'

'Hopefully. Fingers crossed.'

Grace smiled. 'That poem you mentioned in class?' Sarah nodded. 'If you'd like me to have a look at it.'

'Would you?' Sarah said. 'I wouldn't feel comfortable reading it out in class. It's very personal.'

Grace nodded. 'I understand. Have you got it with you?'

'No. I could bring it in.'

Grace popped on her glasses. 'Why don't you pop it around to my flat.' She took out a piece of paper and wrote her address on it. 'If I'm not in just pop it through the letterbox.'

Sarah took the paper from her. 'I will.'

Grace pulled open the drawer in front of her and stared down at Sarah's journal. 'There's something else.'

Sarah stepped nearer. The door to the classroom opened, and a woman popped her head inside. 'Sorry to interrupt, Grace. There's a telephone call for you.'

'Can you take a message?' Grace said.

'They did say it was important,' the woman said.

Grace hesitated for a moment, looked down at the book, and closed the drawer. 'We'll speak later,' she said to Sarah. 'It'll keep.' Sarah nodded at her and left.

Grace focused on the woman at the door again. 'Can you put it through next door, Abi?'

The woman nodded and left.

Grace stood and pondered for a moment. She re-opened the drawer and picked up the diary, placing it inside her bag.

CHAPTER TWENTY-TWO

FEBRUARY 2015 - Grace opened an eye and groaned at the clock on the bedside cabinet to her right. The doorbell sounded again. She sighed loudly and swinging her feet around, planted them on the floor. Making her way unsteadily towards the door, she grabbed her dressing gown as she exited the bedroom. The bell sounded again.

'I'm coming,' she murmured under her breath. She reached the door and opened it. Sarah stood outside smiling.

'Sarah?' Grace said.

'I didn't wake you did I?' Sarah said.

Grace waved her inside. 'I was out last night. Drinking of the grape.'

Sarah smiled. 'Feeling a bit delicate?'

'Extremely. Coffee?'

Sarah nodded, closed the door behind her and followed Grace into the kitchen. Grace filled the kettle and prepared the cafetiere. She pointed for Sarah to sit and slumped in a chair opposite. 'We didn't arrange to meet did we?' Grace said.

'No. Ben's doing a job for a friend. He doesn't normally work Sundays, and I was at a bit of a loose end. You don't mind?'

Grace stood and made the coffee. 'No. Not at all. A large cup of this.' Raising high the coffee pot. 'And I'll be human again.' She opened a cupboard and pulled two large cups from it placing them on the table in front of Sarah.

Sarah opened her bag and pulled out a piece of paper. 'I know you won't feel up to reading it now, but I've brought the poem I told you about.'

Grace held out her hand and took it from her. 'No time like the present.' She stood and searched the room. 'Do me a favour, Sarah. Fetch my glasses from the lounge. They'll either be on the arm of a chair or in the coffee table drawer.

Sarah stood. 'You should eat. You look a little pasty.'

'I'll make some toast.' Standing, she trudged across to the fridge. 'Coffee and toast usually put me right.'

Sarah smiled and left the kitchen. Grace slotted two pieces of bread into the toaster and placed her hands on the worktop waiting for them to pop up. She turned as Sarah came back. 'Have you eaten?'

Sarah stood at the threshold of the door and glared. Grace's eyes lowered to Sarah's hand. The journal grasped tightly between Sarah's fingers, her knuckles white. Grace stared at her. Words she wanted to say, words she needed to say stalled in her throat. The toast popped up, Grace briefly glanced back at it.

'It's not what you think.' She managed to coax from her mouth. The words lacking any conviction.

'You took it,' Sarah said. A mixture of anger and sadness clouded her features.

'I—' Grace slumped onto a seat.

'You know what it means to me. You know how important it is. Why would you …?'

Grace put a hand over her mouth, lowering her eyes she slowly shook her head. 'I …' She closed her eyes. A thick cloud descended her thoughts, masking the words she desperately sought. Words in all honesty Grace knew would be inadequate.

'This is me inside here.' Tapping her fingers on the book. 'These are my private thoughts. No one was meant to see them. They're part of me. My soul laid bare.' She held out the book with a trembling hand.

Grace stood and edged towards her. 'Sarah—'

Sarah held up her hand to ward off Grace. 'I thought we were friends.'

'We are, Sarah. It was an aberration.' Grace stepped closer. 'I don't know why I did it. I can't explain.'

Sarah shook her head. 'If you had asked ... I may have shown you …. I respected you, Grace. I thought maybe in time we could become close friends.'

'We can, we—'

'I'm angry Grace. Angry and so sad. I feel … like Aaron made me feel.' Sarah brought a hand to her mouth and gasped. Clutching the book tightly against her chest.

Grace stepped closer still and held out her hand. 'I didn't mean any of this. I took it and realised it was wrong. I didn't know how to get it back to you without you knowing. I was going to tell you about it when you came back after the class.'

Sarah scowled. 'Did you read it?'

Grace lowered her eyes.

Sarah spun around and marched for the door. Grace following after her as Sarah stormed outside into the torrential rain now falling.

Grace caught hold of her arm as they neared her car. 'Please Sarah, don't leave like this.' Huge droplets of water cascaded down her face.

Sarah shrugged off Graces grip and fumbled for her car key in her bag.

Grace held out her hand again, Sarah swatted it away. Her hair now bedraggled. She whirled around to face Grace as the car keys slipped from her grasp.

Grace bent to retrieve them. Sarah grabbed her arm pushing her away. 'Leave them!' Sarah said. Grace recoiled. Sarah scooped them back up and glared at Grace. 'If this is what's important.' Holding up her book. 'Have it.' Sarah almost spat the words. Her eyes now swamped with tears.

Grace watched as the journal was tossed and skidded to a halt on the road. She rushed to retrieve it, narrowly avoiding being hit by a passing vehicle. She jumped back as the car ran over the book. Kneeling on the wet floor, Grace picked up the now tattered pages. She stood and turned as Sarah's car sped off. Racing indoors she tossed the book onto the hall table and leapt upstairs. Pulling on jogging bottoms and a sweatshirt, she bounded downstairs, pushed on a pair of plimsoles, grabbed her car keys and set off after Sarah.

She followed Sarah onto the dual carriageway. Sarah some way in front. Grace, her eyes glued to the bright-red vehicle in the distance, accelerated further and realising Sarah was getting away from her, screamed in frustration. Weaving and dodging between cars and vans in an effort to close the gap, and ignoring her own safety, she sped on. The wipers furiously trying to wash away the deluge from the windscreen. Grace leant forward and peered out desperately trying to decipher the way ahead. Reds lights in front of her appeared from nowhere, and Grace reacting quickly slammed on the brakes. Her car skidded along the wet tarmac and came to a halt inches from a van in front. She surveyed the carnage ahead. A jumble of vehicles strewn across the road filled her vision.

'Sarah,' she said. Grace fought to release herself from the seatbelt. She turned and reached for the door handle as another car ploughed into the back of her car. Grace was flung forward, her head connecting with the dashboard. She sat up straight and put her hand to her temple. The stickiness of blood clung to her fingertips. She pushed open the door, the car groaned metallically as she tumbled out. She clumsily stood, her vision blurred, a mixture of rain and blood running down her forehead and into her eyes. She stumbled forward. Catching sight of the red car up ahead. It's shape a mangled mess. She staggered on past static vehicles, some undamaged and others a crumpled mess. Her head swam, dizziness swamped her thoughts as she struggled to stay upright. She reached out and sagged against a car. Her legs now unable to support her as Grace fell to her knees, against the door of the vehicle. She looked up. Sarah's car agonisingly close to her as she tumbled forward and slumped onto her side. The rain from above washing over her as she struggled to stay conscious. Grace closed her eyes against the stinging liquid as she plummeted headlong into the darkness.

CHAPTER TWENTY-THREE

Constrict my throat and ache my heart.
Pull senses back through time's deep sea.
And drown me in waters of long-suppressed.
In a bottomless ocean of self-pity.
And nothing can resist its strength.
Or free me from its iron-clad grip.
The dagger-like stab of memories past.
Unwelcome fall, defences strip.
Laid bare before this mighty force.
A locus where raw power resides.
I give up hope, embrace despair.
As dreams are washed away on tides.
Nothing good is left for me.
My sanity stares, fragile and brittle.
I fall supine and beg forgiveness.
Subsumed by guilt, I die a little.

Grace lay on her side in the hospital bed. The door opened and someone walked in. She remained motionless, her face towards the wall.

The nurse strode across to the window and threw open the curtains. 'How are we feeling?'

She peered at the uniformed woman and sat up. 'I've got a massive headache.' She closed her eyes as pain shot across her temple.

The nurse held out a plastic container with two capsules inside. 'Take these. They'll help with that.'

Grace poured the tablets into her hand and tossed them into her mouth. Washing them down with a beaker of water. 'Any news on the woman from the accident?'

'Did you know her?'

Grace shook her head. 'No. I just heard about her.'

'I'm afraid she died,' the Nurse said. 'Her injuries were severe.'

Grace looked away and fixed her stare somewhere in space as she digested the news.

The nurse moved towards the door. 'You should be ok to go home later. The Doctor's on his rounds now. Would you like some breakfast?'

Grace shook her head, and the nurse left. She lay on her side and pulled her legs to her chest. Tightly hugging her knees as tears slowly tumbled from her.

Ben stood inside the waiting room as the news about Sarah sunk in. The doctor gave his apologies, and after asking Ben if he would like to speak with someone, which Ben declined, the doctor left. His mind drifted back through the years to his first wife and her death. The feelings he had now, mirrored them. He put a hand inside his jacket pocket and pulled out a jewellery box. It's presence now no longer a joy, only a stark reminder of his loss. He resisted the temptation to throw it against the wall. A mixture of frustration and anger welling inside him. He stroked the box and returned it to his pocket. The door opened, and Mary strode in. She scrutinised her brother. A pained expression spread across her face. Ben dropped his head and slowly shook it. Mary stopped. Her hand shot up to cover her mouth. She raced across and took hold of her brother as tears pooled in her eyes.

'I don't know what to say, Ben,' she whispered. 'I'm so very sorry.' And hugged him tight.

Ben stared at her, his face drawn and pale. 'What's the point in searching for happiness, Mary? If this is what lives at the end of the journey.'

Mary closed her eyes unable to stop her tears as they pushed their way out. Cascading the length of her face and dripping onto the floor.

The nurse stopped at the door with Ben and Mary. 'Take as long as you want.'

Ben nodded, and as Mary took hold of his arm, they entered.

Sarah lay on a bed. A sheet stretched from over her feet to under her chin. Her face hardly marked at all save for a bruise on the side of her forehead. Ben crept closer as he freed himself from his sister's grip. Mary remained at the foot of the bed. He reached the side of Sarah and tilted his head a little lifting his huge hand to rest on her cheek. Bending, he placed the gentlest of kisses on her blue-tinged lips. He turned and took hold of Mary's hand, stopping at the threshold for one final glimpse of Sarah, and then exited.

Ben, carrying Sarah's effects and holding onto Mary's hand, was met by Toby. Trudging silently outside and across to the carpark the three of them climbed into the vehicle and travelled to his sister's house. The journey a silent one.

Grace sat up as she heard the door to her room open and a nurse enter.

'You've got a visitor,' she said. 'Your friend, Lucy.'

Grace closed her eyes and looked away. 'I don't want to see anyone.'

'She's been waiting a while.'

Grace sighed and opened her eyes again. 'I don't want to see anyone. In any case, I'll be going home shortly.'

'If you're sure?'

'I am.' Grace winced. Her headache from this morning pushing its way forward again.

The nurse left as Grace closed her eyes again and tried to think of anything but the accident. Anything but Sarah. She opened them once more as she heard voices from outside. One of which she recognised was Lucy.

'I'll only be a few minutes,' Lucy pleaded.

'She's adamant,' the nurse said.

'One minute … thirty seconds, that's all.'

The door opened, and Grace listened as it shut behind whoever entered. Someone eased onto a chair next to her bed. Grace didn't move. Her back to Lucy.

'I told them I didn't want to see anyone,' Grace said.

'I know you did.'

Grace shrugged turning around to face her friend.

Lucy forced a smile. 'Ricky's waiting outside.'

'I can't see him.'

'Why? What's wrong?'

Grace turned away again as a sob erupted in her mouth. Her vain attempt at stifling it, thwarted.

Lucy stood and ambled around to the other side of the bed. She wrapped her arms around Grace and pulled her close. 'Tell me what's wrong.'

'I've done something terrible.' Grace sobbed and covered her eyes with her hands. 'I've done ….' Her voice trailed off into a whimper. Her search for the right words a hopeless endeavour.

Grace told Lucy everything. Having persuaded her she couldn't see Ricky yet, the pair journeyed home in Lucy's car. The trip almost devoid of conversation as the friends exchanged glances with each other. Lucy pulled the car up outside Grace's flat.

Grace opened the passenger door, and Lucy grabbed hold of her arm. 'Are you sure you don't want to stay with us? Just for a couple of days?'

Grace nodded. 'I'm sure.' She mouthed a thank you and got out. Lucy watched as Grace plodded inside before driving away.

Grace stripped and tossed her clothes into the washing machine. She showered. The water fiery hot compared to her usual lukewarm one. She dressed, made herself a cup of tea, and slumped into an armchair. Her guilt a seething, hectoring presence, preventing her mind from travelling anywhere but the accident. Sarah's face glared back at her. A mixture of sadness and betrayal ingrained within it. Glancing across at the table in the dining room, she closed her eyes and swallowed a lump which appeared from nowhere and stalled in her throat. She put down her tea, stood, and trod over to the table. The journal lying on top of it screamed at her. Stretching out a hand she picked it up pulling it close. She marched towards the kitchen and pressed the lever of the pedal bin. The book precariously held between a finger and thumb. Grace paused before allowing the lid to drop back down. She trudged back into the dining room and opening a drawer, paused again. The book clung to Grace, her hand unable to let go of it. The front, a picture with flowers on it, battered by the wheels of the car. She opened the book and began to read. *The Journal of Sarah ...'* She dropped to her knees as the gathering storm of grief wrapped itself around her, swirling, smashing its way to her core. It's ferocity matched by the pain within her which rose from the depths of her stomach and crashed into her chest. She fell to the floor, curling into a ball, the book clutched tightly to her. Both an aberration and a comfort. Her guilt growing to massive proportions, engulfed her completely, as she tumbled headfirst, helplessly, into a black hole of sadness.

Grace stood and plodded towards the door, her leaden feet, labouring over the short journey. She opened it. Ricky stood outside his face etched with worry. He silently followed her into the lounge as Grace slumped in an armchair.

Ricky forced a smile, its appearance unconvincing as he sagged down opposite her. 'I was worried. Worried after the accident. Worried that you didn't want to see me.'

'I'm all right.'

'I thought that bump on the head you received, might have put you off me.' He forced another smile and held out his hands. 'Lucy said you didn't want to see anybody. Why wouldn't you want to see me?'

Grace turned her face from him. She felt tearful but pushed the emotion away. She coughed, her resolve bolstered. 'I think we should maybe have a break from each other.'

Ricky lifted his head and stared at her. 'But I thought …'

Grace stood to face him. 'It's not working, Ricky.'

Standing he moved to reduce the gap between them. Grace held out a hand. 'Please,' she said. 'Don't make this any harder.'

'I thought we had something going. Something special.'

She pulled the ring from her finger and placed it on the arm of her chair. Ricky stared at it. The stone within it catching the light as a shaft of sunshine slid across the room.

'I'm sorry.' She stepped back. Putting distance between herself, the ring, and Ricky.

He stepped forward and picked up the ring. He gazed down at it seated in the palm of his hand. 'If it's something I've said or done. I'm sorry … If I've upset you in some way?'

Grace shook her head. 'No. You've done nothing.'

'I love you, Grace. You must know that.'

Grace turned away from him and stared at a point in space. 'You should go.'

Ricky took a step towards her but faltered. He turned and strode towards the door, stopping at the threshold for a final look, and then he was gone. Grace spun around and viewed the empty space Ricky once occupied. She brought her hands to her face and sobbed. Her tears unlike any shed before.

Lucy followed Grace through into the kitchen. Grace flicked on the switch to the kettle. She stood staring at the wall, her friend's eyes boring a hole in her back.

'How are you?' Lucy said.

'Fine.'

'Ricky came around to see me.'

'How is he?' Grace said.

'Concerned. Confused. He doesn't understand why the woman he adores, the woman who agreed to marry him, is acting this way.'

'You didn't tell him, did you?'

'Of course not. I promised you I wouldn't.'

Grace tilted her head upwards. 'I couldn't bear it if he knew.'

'It was an accident. You can't go on blaming yourself.'

Grace shakily picked up the kettle as it clicked off. Her hand hovering above the cups. 'It was my fault. Sarah …' She closed her eyes as the name conjured up an image. 'She would be alive if it wasn't for me. Ben would still have a wife. Nothing you or anyone else says will alter that.'

'But why Ricky? He would understand.'

'I can't be happy, Lucy. Not now. Not ever.'

'That's silly.' She walked across to her friend. Took the kettle from Grace and placed it back on its stand. Grace turned to face her. Tears tumbling down her face like melting ice.

'I've spoiled something beautiful and special.' Her hand shot up to her mouth. Lucy hugged her close. Gently rocking Grace in her arms. Her friend's sobbing the only sound in the quietness of the room.

CHAPTER TWENTY-FOUR

JUNE 2015 – Grace tidied the shelves. Turning as the door to the shop opened.

Ben marched in. 'Everything ok?'

Grace smiled. 'Very well. We've had a good day.'

'Great. I'll treat you to coffee.'

'How about something stronger. I fancy a glass of wine.'

'Wine? A glass of wine it is.'

'I'll finish cashing up, and then I'll be with you,' Grace said.

Ben pulled down the shutter of the shop and locked it, turning to face Grace. 'Where do you fancy?'

She pointed over the road. 'The Sidewinder?'

Ben's smile fell from his face. 'I'd rather go somewhere else. If that's ok?'

Grace mentally admonished herself for her stupidity. 'Of course. You choose.'

Grace peered up as Ben placed a glass of wine in front of her and eased down opposite.

'I've looked forward to this all day,' she said.

He sipped at his pint. 'The beers not fantastic here but it'll do.'

'The Sidewinder … I'm sorry, I forgot.'

Ben's shoulders slumped as he dropped down his eyes. 'Sarah and I used to go there a lot. After she died I …'

Grace nodded. 'I see. I didn't mean to pry.'

'You're not. It's just I haven't been in since.'

Grace lowered her gaze. The guilt she felt rose within her. 'How did she …?' The words stumbled clumsily from her. Asking him a question she already knew the answer to seemed so wrong. Like betrayal.

'A car crash.'

Grace tried to speak but couldn't. A lump the size of a golf ball lodged in her throat. She nodded, trying desperately to stop the tears forming in her eyes from developing further.

'The huge accident on The Parkway last year. I don't know if you remember it?'

Grace frowned deeply. Reaching into her handbag, she plucked a tissue from it and blew her nose. 'I'm sorry.'

Ben put a hand on hers. 'Are you ok?'

'I was involved in that.'

'I'm sorry, Grace. I didn't mean to upset you.'

Grace bit down on her lip. How could he be so compassionate to her after what she'd done? Grace wanted to tell him everything. Bare her soul and beg for his forgiveness. How could she sit here and lie to him? She felt nauseous and fought the urge to flee.

'Bad memories.' She managed to offer up.

Ben moved closer and put an arm around her. 'I'm sorry.'

Grace found resolve from somewhere. Pushing the guilt back deep inside herself she forced a smile. 'It's me who should be sorry. You lost your wife and I'm sat here blubbing like a schoolgirl.'

'You didn't lose anyone, did you?'

Grace shook her head. 'I suffered a concussion. I don't remember the accident itself. It's thinking about it which upsets me. Silly really. I haven't driven since.'

Ben smiled at her. 'Let's talk about something else.' Grace nodded.

A woman appeared next to Ben and placed a hand on his shoulder. 'Ben.' She beamed. 'How are you?'

'Hi, Mel,' Ben said. 'I'm fine.' He glanced towards Grace. 'This is Grace. She's working at the bookshop with me. I've been struggling to manage on my own.'

Mel smiled pleasantly at Grace. 'Hello. I'm a friend of Ben's sister, Mary.'

'Nice to meet you,' Grace said.

'I thought you drank in the Sidewinder?' Mel said to Ben.

Ben coughed. 'Not so much these days.'

Grace briefly closed her eyes and looked away. The guilt within churned her insides.

'I'm so sorry, Ben,' Mel said. 'I forgot.' She gently stroked his arm as Grace turned back and studied the pair.

Ben glanced in Grace's direction before returning his gaze to Mel. 'I'll have to pop in and see the old gang,' he said. 'What are you doing back here? Mary told me that you were living in Portugal.'

Mel placed her hand on Ben's arm again. 'Only sometimes. I pop back occasionally. I've invited Mary and Toby over. You should come.'

'I might just do that,' he said.

Grace glanced at her watch. 'I should go, Ben. I promised a friend of mine we'd meet later.'

Ben stood. 'I'll drop you off.'

Grace placed a hand on his arm. 'It's fine. I'm meeting her in town.' She studied Mel again. 'Nice to meet you.' And offered her hand.

'Nice to meet you, Grace,' Mel said.

Ben hugged Grace tightly. The pair parted, and Grace wandered off. She stopped outside the pub and viewed the couple inside through the window. Mel squeezed next to Ben. The pair laughing together. Grace dropped her head down, turned and marched off.

Friday 16th — Went for a drink with Ben. I knew sooner or later he'd mention Sarah and how she died, but it took me by surprise. The bad memories I'd tried to suppress returned with a vengeance. I feel such a fraud. Part of me wants to walk away from Ben and let him get on with his life, but another part of me cannot come to terms with what I did. My emotional dichotomy is so confusing. What if Ben discovers Sarah was in my writing class? How will I explain that? I've added more to the ball of guilt living within me. I can't shake the feeling that one day it will crush me.

Saturday 17th — I'm dreading work on Monday. Ben's going to be at the shop first thing, and I don't know if I can face him again. How did I end up here? I hoped I was over the worst, but I feel as if I could curl into a ball and stay like that forever. It's Ben's sadness which spurs me on. What I'm doing is stupid. How can I repair the irreparable? How can I replace the irreplaceable?

Grace finished her meal and slumped onto the settee to watch a movie. She had phoned Lucy earlier and declined the offer of Sunday lunch at her house, claiming she felt slightly unwell. Thankfully, Lucy didn't appear to suspect anything. She didn't want Lucy turning up at her flat and giving her the third degree. Grace was five minutes into the film when her doorbell sounded. She groaned. Not feeling much like talking, but as the bell chimed again, she clambered to her feet and trudged into the hall. When she opened the door, it was Ben who stood outside.

Grace smiled. 'Ben. What are you ...?'

He smiled back. 'Sorry to bother you at home. I won't be at the shop tomorrow morning. I've got an urgent job that's just cropped up. A good friend needs a favour.'

Grace stepped aside. 'Come in.'

'Are you sure?'

'Of course.' Closing the door behind him as Ben stepped through into the hall.

He followed Grace into the kitchen. 'Will you be ok to open up?'

Grace filled the kettle and motioned for Ben to sit, which he did as she busily prepared the cafetiere. 'No problem. Have you got the keys?'

'Thanks for this.' He pulled them from his pocket and placed them on the table.

'You can stay for a coffee?' Grace said.

'Yeah.' He half-smiled. 'I was a little worried about you.'

Grace picked up the kettle and made the coffee. 'Worried?'

'Yesterday … You seemed upset.'

Grace sat opposite and smiled at him. 'I was being silly. A long day, bad night's sleep on Thursday. You know how things sometimes get blown out of proportion. I'm much better now.'

Ben smiled. 'Good.'

Grace looked him in the eyes and placed a hand on his. 'You can talk to me … about Sarah I mean. You lost your wife, I only got a bump on the head.'

'I've avoided talking about it to anyone. I lost my first wife you see. Quite a while ago. It took me such a long time to recover from her death. I did the counselling bit, and that helped some, but I didn't want to go through all that stuff again.'

'Oh Ben. I had no idea.' Grace squeezed his hand.

'Mary, my sister, has been great but I know …'

Grace squeezed his hand again. 'I can listen. You can tell me if you want.'

Ben forced a smile. 'You're very kind Grace. But I wouldn't want to burden you with …'

'Don't be silly. We all need to have our story heard.'

'I've avoided talking about it because I know what lies ahead. The dark places I visited when I lost Katherine.'

'Your first wife?'

Ben nodded. 'After she died, I didn't think I'd ever find happiness again. Then Sarah came along.'

Grace felt her bottom lip quiver. She wanted to cry. Wanted to break down the wall she had erected, and allow her guilt, her remorse, to come flooding out. But she couldn't allow Ben to see it. She couldn't let herself falter. She needed to stay strong, for Ben. Grace bolstered her resolve and pushed her feelings back below the surface.

'It must have been hard for you,' Grace said.

Ben lifted his eyes up and viewed Grace. 'Sarah was my life. She was so special. It took me years to part with Katherine's stuff, but when Sarah came along, it seemed the natural thing to do. I won't kid you. It wasn't easy.'

Grace placed a hand on his. 'Of course not.'

Ben shrugged. 'The memories which Katherine and I shared together … when they end up in boxes …'

Ben's eyes filled with tears. Grace pulled her chair nearer to him and put an arm around his massive shoulders. And as he began to sob Grace joined him. Their mutual loss and grief conjoined in an unholy alliance of sorrow.

Grace stirred as Ben slid from the bed. She watched as he pulled on his underwear, jeans and a sweater. She sat up pulling the sheet to her shoulders.

He turned and looked at her. 'I'm sorry about that.'

She forced a smile. 'About what?'

'It was wrong of me. I'm your employer. I should never have come around.'

'I'm a big girl, Ben. You didn't force yourself on me.'

He put his hands to his face and slowly pulled them down. 'You're really nice, but I overstepped the line. I'm still grieving for Sarah. I feel awful.'

'Of course you're grieving for your wife. I understand that. I'm as much to blame as you. I could have stopped it. I didn't want to.'

Ben half-smiled. 'You're very kind, Grace. I should go.'

Grace nodded. 'Ok. This won't affect our working relationship, will it?'

'No. Of course not.' His head dropped lower. 'Thanks for understanding.'

'I'm here if you need to talk. You do know that?' He paused at the door, mouthed a thank you, then turned and left the room. Grace pulled her knees to her chest and listened for the bang of the front door. She rolled onto her side and closed her eyes. Angry she'd allowed this to happen. It was too soon. Ben was still grieving for Sarah, and she had used this to her advantage. What was she thinking? How could she be so stupid? She punched the duvet in frustration, closed her eyes and mentally pleaded for a repeal of time.

CHAPTER TWENTY-FIVE

JULY 2015 - Grace opened the shop and after having an unusually busy day for a Monday, finally slumped into a seat with a cup of tea. After cashing up and programming the new books into the till, she checked the rear of the shop. Satisfied it was locked, she put on her coat. The door opened, and Ben strode in with a bunch of flowers.

He smiled at Grace. 'I owe you an apology.' And handed her the bouquet.

'What for?'

'The appalling way I treated you the other day. It was way out of order. I shouldn't have …'

Grace held up her hand. 'Ben. I was as much, more, in fact, to blame. You're still grieving for your wife. For … Sarah.' Her name struggled clumsily from her mouth. She looked up and blew out hard. 'I shouldn't have taken advantage either. I like you, Ben. A lot.'

'You make me sound so helpless.' He smiled.

'Of course you're not helpless, but …'

'I'm fond of you, Grace. You make me laugh. I don't want to be sad anymore. I've spent a lot of my life wallowing in self-pity. It's an unforgiving land to live in.'

Grace edged closer. 'Maybe I can help a little.'

'If we moved more slowly …'

'Let's make this a friendship for now.' She took hold of his hand.

'Can I buy you dinner?'

'You don't have to.' She smiled.

'I'd like to. As friends.'

'You've spent enough already.' She held up the bouquet. 'We'll share the cost.'

Ben nodded and opened the door allowing Grace to exit. 'There's a new restaurant opened on Albert Road. I've heard good things about it.'

They enjoyed an excellent meal. Ben opened up to Grace about Sarah. On one or two occasions he appeared to her as if he would break down, but somehow he held it together. Ben had brightened up as the meal wore on. Grace trying to lighten the mood throughout. Steering him away from the maudling.

Finally, after finishing their meal, he dropped her off at her flat. A hug and a brief kiss on the cheeks exchanged before she headed inside and Ben drove off.

Grace slumped into the armchair and sighed loudly. Ben was falling for her she was sure. But did she feel the same way about him? She wasn't at all certain. Her mind in turmoil. 'This is what you wanted. This is what you gave up everything for,' she muttered out loud. You wanted him to fall for you. Wanted him to forget his loss of Sarah. Wanted him to be happy again. But something hectored and nagged at her. Something didn't seem right. Her sense of doing the right thing faltered. She got up and opened a drawer in the dresser, pulling out a picture frame she stared at it. The image of herself and Ricky smiled back. Grace put a hand up to her mouth, her eyes full with tears.

'How can you do this?' she said to herself. 'It's people's lives you're messing with.' She returned the photo. Placing it face down, she covered it with a magazine before slamming the drawer shut.

GRACE'S JOURNAL

JULY 20th - I had clarity of thought once. Try and make Ben happy that was my mantra. Now I'm faltering. My doubts are the thoughts which shout the loudest. They demand to be heard. I like Ben. I like him a lot, but I don't love him. Not how I loved …

I may never love him. Ben doesn't deserve this. He doesn't deserve what I'm doing to him. I can't believe I was so stupid. I can't believe I thought that this would work. Lucy was right. This would end badly. Suddenly the world seems alien to me. I don't know what to do. I'm cast adrift in an ocean of doubt.

Grace awoke having endured an unsurprising fitful night's sleep. After showering, she dressed, made breakfast and sat down to eat it. She checked her mobile. Lucy had called and left messages. Grace ignored her friend's calls and resisted the temptation to ring her back. Strangely though, the small amount of sleep she'd managed had cleared her mind. Bringing about a clarity of thought which alluded her the previous night. It appeared her resolve had been bolstered in some way, and it was with a new sense of optimism she set off to work. She remembered Ben had told her he would be working away for a couple of days. Far from being relieved, she missed him. It was as if her mind had ironed out her problems as she slept. And now Grace knew, more than at any time, she and Ben could have a future together. She wouldn't kid herself and believe the coming weeks and months would be easy, but somehow from somewhere, she understood. This is what she wanted.

Grace had spent a busy shift at the shop. A steady stream of customers most of the day had kept her occupied. As she finished cashing up, she could scarcely believe how quickly the hours had passed. She headed off away from the shop and onto Linthorpe Road. Lucy had phoned just after she'd opened and left a voice message, inviting her for a drink after work. After mulling it over for the best part of the morning, she had returned her call and accepted. They hadn't spoken since the day Lucy came into the shop. Grace realising that she couldn't avoid her friend forever, had decided to grasp the nettle. She wouldn't be candid though. She would give Lucy only the barest facts about her and Ben. As far as Lucy was concerned, she would be keeping her cards close to her chest.

Grace stopped outside the wine bar and checked her appearance in the tinted window. A reflection of someone familiar caught her attention and she turned around. Mel stood across the road buried in conversation on her mobile. Grace studied her, but realising she may be spotted ducked behind a bus shelter. A taxi drew up outside, and Ben, another man and a woman got out. She continued to watch the party as Ben exchanged kisses with Mel and they set off inside. Grace stared across as the three of them disappeared into the interior of the restaurant.

'I thought it was you,' Lucy said.

Grace shaken from her reverie turned. 'Hi, Luce.' She hugged and kissed her friend.

'What are you looking at?'

Grace shook her head. 'Nothing. I just thought I recognised somebody.'

Lucy nodded towards the door. 'Shall we?'

'Absolutely,' said Grace. She followed Lucy inside but couldn't resist one final glance across the road, as she and Lucy were conveyed to their table.

CHAPTER TWENTY-SIX

SEPTEMBER 2015 - Five months had passed since Emily and Richard separated. Although she missed him a lot, time had put a distance between herself and the hurt she felt. Her writing not suffering at all, quite the opposite. It appeared enduring sadness is not the worst thing that can happen to a writer. Being able to plumb some of the darker emotions of her psyche had initiated a positive effect on her word count. Near to finishing the book, and more than satisfied with how the narrative played out, she felt pleased, as she waited in the restaurant for Oliver.

She sipped at her wine as Oliver strolled through the doors and across to her table. She stood, meeting him with a kiss before they sat.
'How's my favourite writer?' he said.
'Very well. Did you have a chance to read the chapters I sent you?'
Oliver picked up the menu. 'I did. Loved them. I forwarded them on to Sandersons. I should hear something back this week.'
'I hope they like them,' she said. 'I know it's taken a while.'
'Forget about that. They'll love them. They love you. All I hear from them is, "When will she finish the book?" They're excited.' Oliver patted her hand. 'It'll be worth the wait.'
The waiter appeared pausing with his pen. Oliver glanced up at him. 'I'll have the lamb please.'
'Carbonara,' Emily said.
Oliver smiled. Emily looked at him. 'What?' she said.
'It's all you ever order.'
'Can I get you any drinks?' the waiter asked.
Oliver grabbed the bottle from the ice bucket and inspected it. 'There's plenty here. Madam hasn't drunk it all.' Aiming a smile at Emily.
The waiter nodded, smiled and left.

'Cheeky bugger,' Emily said. 'You'd think I was an alcoholic or something.'

'It takes one to know one,' Oliver said. Pouring himself a glass. He took a long sip and fixed Emily with a stare. 'When is it going to be finished?'

'A week or two.'

'Fantastic.' Raising his glass high. 'Shall we toast to your first million, and my ten-per cent cut of it?'

Emily smiled and clinked glasses with Oliver. 'Yes, I think we should. Cheers.'

Oliver helped Emily along the corridor, stopping outside her room, and fumbled for the keycard.

'I'm sorry, Oliver,' she slurred. 'I'm a little tipsy.'

Finally, the door clicked open and the pair staggered in. 'You were tipsy an hour ago,' he said. 'You're way past tipsy now.' He flicked on the light illuminating the clothes-strewn bedroom.

'Christ, Emily. What the hell happened in here?'

Emily dropped onto the bed and kicked off her shoes. 'I never pretended to be tidy. I like to see what I've brought with me.'

'Well, we can certainly see what you've brought with you. How many months did you intend staying.'

She giggled. 'A girl can never pack enough knickers.'

'Would you like me to make you a strong coffee?' He laughed and flicked on the kettle.

'There's some wine in the fridge,' she said.

Oliver frowned. 'Have you seen the price of the minibar. I think you've had enough already, young lady.'

'Don't be so boring,' she said. 'We're celebrating.'

'You can celebrate too much.'

Emily flopped back on the bed. 'You can stay the night if you want? It's a huge bed.' Patting the side of the bed next to her.

'Well, it was before you covered it in bras and briefs.'

Emily giggled again and brushed them onto the floor. 'There you go. Now it's tidy.'

He slowly shook his head. 'I don't think it's a good idea. We've both had a lot to drink.'

Emily closed her eyes. 'Please yourself. I won't ask a second time.'

Oliver laughed. 'You'll thank me in the morning.' He stared at her. 'Can you manage on your own sweetie?'

Emily didn't answer. Oliver smiled and pulled the duvet across her. He turned, stepping over the contents of Emily's luggage, laughed to himself, and tiptoed across the room. Pausing, he glanced back at the sleeping Emily, shook his head again, switched off the light and exited.

EMILY'S DIARY

September 20th, 2015 - Met Oliver today and had lunch. Had way too much to drink and ended up being put to bed by him. Had a thumping headache in the morning. I telephoned him and apologised. He just laughed. I'm sure I propositioned him. I'm blushing as I write this.

Things with the publishers are going well. I just need a good ending to my story. I've told him I'll have it finished in a week or two. Let's hope I don't let him down.

September 27th 2015 – I won't lie. Writing the ending of my book has been emotionally draining. As a writer, you have to leave something of yourself on the pages, along with sweat and tears. I'm happy with it, but I'm not sure the publishers will be. I've wandered from my original synopsis. But we are affected by what happens around us. There are chips and chinks in us all. Sometimes in life a fault-line opens up, and there's nothing we can do about it. I've emailed the final chapters to Oliver. Que Sera.

CHAPTER TWENTY-SEVEN

AUGUST 2015 - Grace listened for the slightest noise from above, the silence deafened her. Arriving at the top, she reached for the handle and pushed open the door to his flat. It was silent. She half expected voices. The door to the living room wide open, as was the one leading to the kitchen. Only the bathroom and bedroom remained. She pushed open the bathroom door. The creaking of the hinges causing her to catch her breath. This too was empty. She stared at the remaining door. Her heartbeat now banging inside her chest. She wanted to go. Terrified by what lay behind the door. She couldn't leave. She needed to know. Hesitatingly, she tiptoed forward and placed a trembling hand on the doorknob. Gasping for rarefied air and briefly closing her eyes she slowly turned the handle and pushed it open. She gazed up in horror. Ben hanging from the ceiling, a crude noose tied around his neck, his lips tinged blue. She raced to the kitchen, and threw open the door, grabbing a large carving knife from within. She hurried back and began sawing at the rope, the blade suitably sharp, easily sliced through it as Ben's inert body fell to the floor with a thump. She pulled at the noose, loosening it, she slid it over his head and dropped to her knees next to him. Putting her lips to his, Grace blew, pushing two breaths into him. Feeling for a pulse, she paused, there was one. It was faint, but there was one. Reaching for her bag, she pulled out her mobile.

Grace sat observing Ben in the hospital bed, the rise and fall of his chest hypnotic. He stirred. Opening his eye's, he glanced up at the ceiling, and as if sensing Grace's presence turned to face her. A deep frown etched in his features.

She dabbed at the tears tumbling freely down her cheeks. 'Hi,' she said. 'How are you?'

'I'm sorry.' His voice little more than a whisper. 'I'm so sorry.'

'You don't need to explain. I know why you did it. You're not angry, are you?'

'At who?'

'Me. For finding you before …'

'No. I couldn't be angry with you.'

She leant forward and put a hand on his cheek. 'We can't watch you forever. We can't always be there. If you're determined, we, I, can't stop you. But you have people here who love you so much, Ben. Mary, Toby and your nephews. And me.' She put a hand on her stomach. 'Someone in here too.'

'You never said.'

'I was going to tell you when you came back. I was scared. I didn't know how you would react.'

He smiled and sat up in bed. 'I promise you, I won't do anything like that again.'

She leant forward and kissed him. 'Mary and Toby are waiting to see you.' She stood and walked towards the door.

'Thanks,' he said.

She stopped and turned. It's the least I owe you, she thought, rather than said.

FIVE YEARS LATER – Grace woke. She eased herself up in bed and yawned. Glancing to her left, she spotted the piece of paper leaning against the bedside cabinet. Stretching for it she read the message. Smiling to herself, and replacing the note, she jumped from her bed. After showering and changing she dressed in a swimsuit complete with a wrap. Grabbing her sunglasses and beach bag, Grace threw open the patio door. The heat of the sun hitting her instantly as she stepped from the air-conditioned room, and onto the sand. She sauntered across the beach stopping at a lounger beneath a large sunshade. In the distance, she could see Ben. He turned and waved, the boy next to him, waved too. The little girl holding his right hand, let go and ran towards her mother. Grace lifted the child into her arms as she reached her.

'What have you been doing while Mummy slept?' Grace said.

CHAPTER TWENTY-EIGHT

APRIL 2016 - Emily showered and changed. Collecting her ticket from the dining table, she deposited it in her handbag. She paused at the front door, turned and walked into the bedroom, slid open the wardrobe and pulled out a box. Inside were several diaries and on top of these a manila envelope. She picked it up and slipped it into her bag. Returning the box she marched outside, pulling her suitcase behind before jumping into the car.

After parking at the station, and checking the departures, she boarded her train just in time. The roadworks on the way to the station slowing her down considerably. Quickly locating her seat, Emily slumped down and pulled the envelope from her bag. She read the letter inside. Although tears formed in her eyes, they didn't fall this time. She refolded the letter, placed it back in the envelope, and put it away. Outside, commuters and travellers clambered onto the Darlington to Kings Cross train. Emily blinked back the unshed tears and closed her eyes as leaden tiredness swept over her.

She woke an hour or so later, wandered along to the buffet car, and bought a sandwich and a cup of coffee. She returned to her seat for the remainder of the familiarly tedious journey.

She was reading a magazine as the train pulled in to the station. Collecting her luggage, she got off. Quickly locating a taxi, and giving the driver the address of her hotel, she slumped back in her seat. Watching the swarm of rush-hour traffic buzz by. It had been a long time since she'd visited London. Not since her last day of work had she stepped a foot here. Her former existence sweeping through her as memories, some good, many not, filled her head. After what seemed an age, she reached her destination. Paying the driver, she stood outside and gazed up at the building. The hotel was nice. A newly built edifice decked in stone and glass. She smiled, took hold of her suitcase, and strode inside.

I flopped onto the bed and groaned. There was a time I hated hotels like this. Encased, cut-off from the real world. There's something false about hotels. A brief holding place for misplaced souls. When you are on your own, it's the loneliness which gets to you. Every conversation, whether with another guest, or staff member, seems forced. Unnatural. It's different when you're with someone, of course. On holiday or such like. But hotels like this one are replete with professional people. Lonely, lost entities with brief-cases. I had come to the end of my journey. Months of writing and re-writing had brought me to this place. The ideas which had bubbled in my head, now ink on paper. I thought of Richard today. His smiling face ambled across my mind. I shed a tear for him and what might have been. A long time has passed since I did that. It gave me a brief respite. Crying, I feel, purges us in some way. The emotions that build up against a dam of resistance are finally breached. The gap existing between the first cry and the next, the hardest to bear. The tears, when they arrive, often welcome. And within the tears, bookended between them, the most challenging area of all. It's this place which is the hardest to traverse. *The space between our tears.*

After unpacking, she gathered her handbag and set off downstairs. Oliver stood waiting for her as she reached reception. The pair kissed and embraced.
'Good journey?' he asked.
'Not bad. I slept most of the way.'
'We're early. Our meeting isn't until twelve. How about we grab a coffee?'
Emily nodded. 'I could do with one. I didn't sleep well last night. A bit of nerves I think.'
'What's to be nervous about? They love you.'
Emily pointed towards a room to her right. 'Shall we?'

The pair sat at a table as a waiter joined them. 'Can I get you something?'
Oliver looked at Emily. 'A skinny latte, please,' she said.
'I'll have an Americano, please,' Oliver said. 'And a small Brandy.'
The waiter nodded, thanked them, and left them to it.
Emily smiled. 'The hotels nice.'
'That's how highly they rate you. You shouldn't be nervous. You should be excited.'
'I am. It's just a little unnerving. What did you think of the ending?'

Oliver clasped his hands together. 'I loved it. It wandered from your original storyline though.'

'What about Sandersons?'

'Don't know, but this is a good sign. They don't normally pull you into the smoke until they're reasonably happy.'

Emily glanced down at the table and then at Oliver. 'Do you think they'll ask for changes?'

Oliver smiled. 'Possibly.'

'Have they discussed anything with you?'

'No, not really.'

The waiter returned, placing the drinks on the table. 'Can I get you folks anything else?'

Emily shook her head as Oliver addressed him. 'I think we're fine, thanks.' The waiter nodded and left.

'I don't want to change anything,' Emily said.

'Emily.' Oliver tapped her on the knee. 'You know the law of writing. Don't fall in love with your words. The thing is to get this book published. You're a first-time writer. You have—'

Emily leant back in her chair. 'You wouldn't understand.'

Oliver forced a smile. 'Let's see what they have to say first. All I'm saying is, be flexible.

Emily rubbed her eyes. She felt drained already. Her sleepless night, the long journey, helping to sap her strength. But it was more than that. Finishing the book, saying goodbye to her characters, had been incredibly hard to do. The last chapter, the last page, so final.

'I know I can't make demands,' she said. 'I know I'm lucky I'm in this position, but …'

Oliver inched closer. 'Is everything all right?' Taking hold of her hand.

Emily forced a smile. 'Forget it. I'm being silly.'

'If this was your second or third book, Emily … You see what I'm saying?'

'Of course.'

'This could launch a successful career. I know money isn't everything, but …'

'Forget it, Oliver.' Picking up her cup, she took a sip. 'I'll be fine. Let's get this book in print. Shall we?'

Oliver patted her hand. 'That's my girl.' Picking up his brandy, he downed it in one. 'To Emily Kirkby. The next big thing.'

Emily smiled outwardly. Inside knowing what she would do. She wouldn't make changes, couldn't make changes, not major ones. If they insisted, she would walk away. Oliver would be livid if she did. But she didn't care. Sod him, she thought. Sod them all. It was her story. Hers to tell. She wouldn't allow anyone to butcher it. Built word by word, tear by tear.

She was shaken from her reverie as Oliver's phone rang. 'Hello,' he said. He listened intently. 'Fifteen minutes … ok.' Hanging up.

He stared at Emily. 'They've pushed our meeting forward. They want us there now.'

Emily took a large sip from her cup and stood. 'What are we waiting for then.'

They jumped in a taxi and headed over to Sanderson Publishers, arriving there ten minutes later. After presenting themselves to reception, they were escorted upstairs and into an office. A woman behind a desk, stood, and offered her hand.

Oliver smiled at Emily and gestured to the woman. 'You already know Helena, don't you?'

Emily shook her hand. 'Yes. We've spoken on the phone.'

Helena indicated for them to sit. 'I'll have drinks sent in.' Picking up her phone she dialled. 'Sarah,' she said. 'Can you rustle up some drinks please?'

Emily smiled to herself. The name conjuring never-forgotten memories.

Helena took out a file and placed it in front on the desk. 'Giles is going to be joining us. He insisted on it, actually.'

Oliver looked at Emily. 'Giles is Helena's boss.'

'He's excited to meet you,' Helena said.

A young woman entered carrying a tray with tea and coffee pots, and placed it down.

'Thanks, Sarah,' Helena said. The young woman left.

The three of them chatted pleasantly for several minutes before a man joined them.

'Emily, Oliver, this is Giles,' Helena said.

Giles held out a hand. 'Oliver,' he said. 'I think we've met once.' Oliver rubbed his chin. Giles continued. 'At the launch of Annabel Callander's book.'

'Of course,' Oliver said. 'Last year.'

'And this must be Emily?' Giles said. He offered a hand. Emily shook it before the four of them took their seats.

Helena opened the folder in front of her. 'We've read your draft. It's excellent.' Looking across at Giles who nodded. She flicked through the file and took out a piece of paper.

'But ...?' Emily said.

Giles and Helena smiled. 'It did wander a little from your original storyline,' Helena said.

'I won't change it,' Emily said. 'I can't.' Vigorously shaking her head.

Oliver glared at Emily. 'What Emily means—'

155

'Please, Oliver,' she said.

Giles stroked his chin and held up a hand. He peered over the top of his glasses across at Emily. 'Let Emily talk.'

Emily lowered her head. 'It's hard to explain.'

Helena glanced at Giles. 'I know it's difficult when you've written the words,' she said. 'But surely you understand. Even the most experienced of writers make changes.'

Emily raised her head a little, and slowly shook it.

'We thought,' Giles said. 'The Grace character ...' Glancing across at Helena's piece of paper. '... would end up with Ricky. He's the love of her life. I know she felt sorry for Ben. Guilty for what happened to his wife but—'

Tears pooled in Emily's eyes. She dropped her head down. 'I couldn't let him die again. Even if it was only between the pages of a book. I couldn't. I just couldn't.'

Giles glanced at Helena and then back at Emily. 'I don't understand, Emily,' he said

Helena narrowed her eyes. 'Are you saying Ben and Sarah are—'

'Were,' Emily said. 'Were real. Ben and Sarah Stainton were real people. Ben was a carpenter, like in the book. Sarah, his wife, was killed in a car accident.'

Giles rubbed his chin again. 'And the character Grace? Was she real too?'

'My middle name,' she said. 'Emily Grace Kirkby.'

Helena frowned at Oliver, her brow a deep furrow. 'Did you know about this?' she asked.

Oliver shook his head.

'No one knows,' Emily said.

Giles leant forward. 'Are you saying ... all of what happened in the book, *really* happened?'

'More or less. Apart from the ending.'

Helena's eyes widened. 'What happened?'

Emily lowered her head, and Giles tapped her hand. 'Take your time, Emily.'

Emily sagged in her chair. 'I sat on a wall outside Ben's flat while he took his own life.' She half-laughed. 'I sat there wondering if I should knock. Frightened he was in there with another woman. Afraid I would catch them together.' Emily brought a hand to her mouth to stifle a sob. 'When I finally summoned the courage to go inside ... It was too late. Ben Stainton hanged himself.' She uttered the words for the first time in her life.

Giles rubbed his face. 'I see.'

'I'm so sorry,' Emily said. 'Sorry I lied to you all. But in truth, I lied to myself.'

Helena glanced first at Oliver and then back at Giles. 'We'll need a minute or two.'

Emily reached into her handbag and pulled out the envelope. 'You may want to read this.' Handing Helena the note. 'I'll wait outside.' She stood, trudged towards the door, and left.

'I'm sorry,' Oliver said. 'I knew nothing of this.'

'It's still a good story,' Giles said.

Helena blew out. 'But the ending?'

Giles took the envelope from her and taking out the letter, began to read.

Dear Emily,

The fact you're reading this letter means I've been successful at taking my own life. I'm so very sorry. It's an awful thing I do, I know. I realise the upset I will cause to the people I leave behind.

I never planned it this way. Things in life have a way of unfolding differently from what you imagined. When my first wife Katherine died, it was devastating. She had been a massive part of my life for such a long time. I never truly believed I would ever get over her. Then I met Sarah. This timid creature who blew me away and slowly, piece by piece, put my heart back together.

When she died, it felt just like losing Katherine all over again. Only much, much, worse. I refused to wallow in self-pity this time though and pushed my grief to one side.

When you came into my life, Emily, I wasn't looking for anyone else. But you had a way of making me feel happy again. You captivated me. I knew it was very soon after Sarah's death, and maybe it was my state of mind which allowed me to fall for you. I wrestled with my conscience for what seemed like an eternity, but in reality, wasn't very long at all. I decided that I would do with Sarah's belongings, what I had done with Katherine's.

I didn't tell Mary, Toby or my friends. I felt guilty that I was prepared to move on so soon after Sarah's death, and others wouldn't understand. But I knew what lay ahead if I didn't. I couldn't handle years of mourning for another lost love. If this seems selfish, I don't care. When you've spent a large part of your life sad, you have to grab happiness when it appears.

I decided to box up Sarah's things and put them in the attic to await a day when I could part with them for good. It was during this time I discovered an envelope with Sarah's handwriting on it. She must have left it for me on the day of the accident. I'd started work early and missed it. It had somehow been mixed with some other paperwork belonging to her.

When I opened it, I found a card inside. On the front, a picture of a dove, the symbol of hope, and something special to the two of us. Within the card there wasn't any writing but taped to it was a positive pregnancy test.

My world collapsed, and at that moment, I knew what I had to do. Sarah and I had struggled for so long for a baby, and this small piece of plastic was enough to dismantle my defences and bring them tumbling down.

I hope you understand why I did what I did. I hope you can find it in your heart to forgive me.

Along with this letter I've left Sarah's journals. I hope by reading them you can begin to understand what I once had, and ultimately lost. I tried reading them at one time but gave up. Her words were heart-breaking to me.

I wish you well, Emily. I don't honestly know the depth of feelings you had for me, but what I do know, what I sincerely hope, is that you'll find happiness. Some people never find true love in their lives, but I was lucky enough to discover it twice. Something only now, I truly understand.

Good luck, Emily. Good luck on finding that special someone who will steal your heart and make every waking moment with them seem like a lifetime.

Your very good friend.
Ben x.

Emily slumped outside on a chair. Her thoughts drifting endlessly from Sarah to Ben and back again. The door to the office opened, and Oliver popped his head out. 'Do you want to come in?' he said.

Emily stood and followed Oliver into the office, sitting back in her chair.

Giles smiled. His eyes a puffy red. 'The ending stays as you wrote it, Emily.'

Emily brought a hand to her mouth. 'Thank you.' Tears rolled down her cheeks. 'Can I ask one more thing? Can I change their names?'

Giles glanced at Helena. 'Of course,' he said. 'Did you have any in mind.'

She shook her head. 'Not really. It doesn't matter as long as their anonymity is maintained. I think they deserve that.'

'I think so too,' he said.

Oliver and Emily stopped outside the building, she turned to face him. 'I'm sorry about that. Sorry I never warned you.'

He hugged her. 'Don't worry. I forgive you.'

She jumped in a taxi and headed back to the hotel. Although a night had been booked, she didn't feel much like staying. She packed, caught another cab to the station, and headed for home.

CHAPTER TWENTY-NINE

SEPTEMBER 2017 - Emily hurried around the shop in readiness for its opening. The coffee machines were up and running, having finally mastered how to work them. She paused and viewed the counter, satisfied she performed a slow pirouette. Taking in the ambience of the interior she smiled to herself and wandered across to the shelves stacked with books adorning the other three walls. The door opened and Lucy entered holding a child's hand.

He raced across to his mother, Emily, who lifted him into her arms. 'What have you been up to, Ben?'

'Auntie Lucy bought me a lolly,' he said.

Emily motioned around the room. 'What do you think, Luce?'

'It looks fabulous,' Lucy said.

'Thanks.' She kissed her son before placing him down. Ben ran towards one of the corners, its shelves brimming with children's books.

Lucy nodded over her shoulder. 'The guys with the sign have arrived.'

'Thank God.' She headed outside to be greeted by two men busy removing items from the back their van.

Emily joined them. 'Is it finished?'

'It is,' said the elder of the two men. 'And even if I say so myself, it looks superb.'

'How long will it take you to put up?'

'Fifteen minutes,' he said. 'Enough time for you to make us a posh coffee on that new machine of yours.' He nudged his mate playfully and winked at her.

She laughed. 'Ok,' she said. 'What about a bacon bun to go with your posh coffee?'

The elder man glanced at his younger friend who nodded his approval. 'That'd be fantastic.' Emily turned and headed back inside.

Emily, holding Ben's hand, led Lucy and Tim outside. The workmen busily placing the last of their stuff in the back of the van. The older man turned and ambled across to Emily.

'What do you think?' he said.

Emily stared up at the sign. Bright red lettering on a black background spelt out the names. *Ben and Sarah's Coffee and Bookshop.*

Her eyes glistened, as her fingers moved to the dove hanging from the chain around her neck. 'I love it.'

OCTOBER 2017 – Emily stood behind the counter of the shop checking her order with the wholesalers. Satisfied, she pinned it to a clipboard and hung it on the wall near to the phone.

'I'll ring it through later,' she said to Rachel.

Rachel placed a latte in front of a customer. 'Did you remember the large cups?'

'Yeah. I'm pretty sure I've got everything.' Turning to pick up a cup, she held it aloft. 'Think I've earned a coffee.'

The door opened, and a man strolled in making his way across to the counter.

Stopping he smiled at Rachel. 'What can I get you?' she said.

'I've come to have a word with your boss.' Focusing his attention on Emily. Emily, with her back to him, stopped what she was doing as the familiar voice penetrated her mind and threw open a window to her past. She turned, still holding the cup in her hand. Richard stood there. Exactly as she remembered him. If he looked any older, she couldn't tell. He was dressed casually in a pair of jeans, a polo shirt and a navy jacket. His hair slightly longer, a broad smile filling his face.

'Hi,' he said.

'Hi.' A smile appeared on her face as she gazed at him. She held up a cup. 'I was about to take a break and have a coffee. Fancy one?'

Richard nodded. 'I'd love one, and I love your shop. You've done really well.'

'Thanks.'

'I read your book.'

'Who'd have thought it?' She picked up a second cup. 'Me, writing a book.'

'I would have,' Richard said. 'I knew you had it in you. I always believed you could do it.'

Emily smiled. 'Thanks.'

'The characters were brilliant. As if they were real.'

Emily turned and smiled to herself. 'Is it still black with no sugar?'

'Yeah. You remembered.'

'Some things are worth remembering.'

Emily and Richard glanced across at Rachel, aware they were being watched by her. Rachel turned away from their glare.

'Grab a seat in the corner, and I'll be over in a second,' Emily said. Richard nodded and strolled into one of the corners.

Rachel smiled and mouthed a 'Who's he?' at Emily, who tapped the side of her nose, smiled back, and made the drinks.

Emily sat opposite Richard and placed down their coffee's.

'How are you?' Richard said.

'Good. The shops doing well. The book continues to sell.'

'Lucy told me they're talking about a movie.'

'You've spoken with Lucy?'

'We kept in touch, after …'

'She never said.'

'I asked her not to say anything,' Richard said.

'Did she tell you anything else?'

'Like what?'

'About me?'

'The past is dissolved sugar in a cup,' he said. 'The future, the milk in the jug. I nicked that from a book.' He smiled at her.

'Not sure I've read that one.' She smiled back. 'I heard you were working down south somewhere.'

'Isleworth. I've got my own dealership.'

'Wow.' Her eyes widened. 'It's what you always wanted. Does it pay well? Tell me to mind my own business, if you like?'

Richard laughed. 'You've never changed. I always loved your honesty. Yes it does. Lovely house, smart car, great set of friends.'

'This just a flying visit then?'

'Unfinished business.' He put his hand into his pocket and pulled out the ring. Gazing at it he held it out to her. 'Something I needed to do. Something I had to do.'

Emily took it from him. 'You kept it?'

'Of course.'

'I'd have taken it straight to cash for gold,' Emily said.

Richard smiled. 'I never stopped loving you. Never gave up on us.'

'Richard—'

'Please let me finish.' Emily nodded. 'I've wanted to come back for months, but I was scared. Scared by what you'd say. There's been no one else. How could there be? I needed to know one way or another if I … we … could make this work. My life is great. I've got everything I'd ever dreamed of, but it's missing one thing. *You.*'

Emily picked up a napkin and squeezed her eyes shut. 'I couldn't move, Richard. My life is in Middlesbrough. My memory's, the good and the bad, reside here.'

162

'Then I'll have to move back.'

'I couldn't ask you to do that.'

'You're not,' he said. 'I've already been sounded out by someone who wants to buy my business. He's offered me a good price. I told him I'd think about it.'

'You'd give up everything for—'

'But look at what I'd get in exchange. I never stopped thinking about you. You were always there. I carried you everywhere with me. In here.' He placed a hand against his heart.

'I hoped you'd come back,' she said. 'But what I did to you was unforgivable.'

'I forgive you. I forgave you a long time ago.' He leant across to her. She held out her hand, and Richard took hold of it. The door to the shop opened and Lucy walked in with Ben. The boy ran across to his mother and jumped up onto her knee, grinning at Richard.

Emily smiled. 'Richard. I'd like you to meet your son.'

NOVEMBER 2017 – Richard perched on the pew, and glanced over his shoulder nervously.

'What time is it?' he said to his best man, Chris.

'Stop worrying,' Chris said. 'She hasn't done a runner.'

Richard squeezed his son's hand. 'Daddy,' Ben said. 'Will mummy have her special dress on?'

'I hope so,' Richard said. 'It cost enough.'

The organist struck up, and Richard, Ben and Chris stood. Richard gazed back along the aisle as the wedding march commenced. Emily, the sun a bright, yellow backdrop, stood in the doorway with Tim. She looked stunning to him as the pair slowly ambled towards the altar. They stopped, and Emily stepped forward to join Richard. He smiled at her, enrapt by her beauty.

'You're gorgeous,' he whispered.

She took hold of his hand and gently squeezed it. 'I love you,' she mouthed as they turned to face the Vicar.

EMILY'S DIARY

December 1st 2017 – This will be my last entry. A new chapter has begun in my life, my old life belongs in the past. It has at times been a long and arduous struggle, but ultimately a rewarding one.

After Ben died, I was gripped by guilt. Guilt for Sarah's death and also Ben's. I'm grateful Ben never knew about my involvement. I don't think I could have endured that. Although knowing Ben, as I did, in the brief time he was in my life, he would forgive me. I could easily have taken a similar route to Ben, and may well have if it wasn't for my son who I was carrying. In a world where love surrounds us, there is one type which trumps all others. One love which sits supreme. A mother's love for her child. This is indeed the greatest of all loves. This diary, along with my others, will be put away with Sarah's, somewhere safe. In the hope that in the future, someone will read them all. And maybe understand not only how precious love is but also how tenuous life can be. I have no more need for journals. I leave this diary with the poem Sarah brought to me on the day she died. It lays bare the terrible life she endured before Ben, and ultimately how he saved her.

My Gilded Cage

With weary head hid deep beneath my tired and broken wing
As gilded tears stung my face, I closed my eyes again
And dreamt of lands beyond my cage, where sunlight warms the day
Where hearts are free to wander, and love can now hold sway
My song no longer mine to have, held fast within my throat
But then I heard a wondrous sound, a sweet melliferous note
He called to me through bars of gold and beckoned me to him
His song a rising mountainous paean, a monumental hymn
With lightning speed, the door was thrown, and liberty was mine
I took to flight and soared with him and left behind my shrine
We flew up high, and sunshine warmed my drab and wounded feathers
No longer held by ropes and chains or life's eternal tethers
With hearts entwined our song found voice as thermals swept us up
And drank the sweetest nectar from his warm and loving cup
We journeyed on, 'cross seas of blue and forests verdant green
And finally dived towards the earth a land of calm serene
He built a bower of finest cloth and furnished it with love
Subsumed within the blinding ray of my majestic dove
I knew by now the shining star whose light would never dim
So tumbled forward, eagerly, sustained by all of him

Emily Grace Kirkby – Mother, Wife, and considerably wiser.

NOTES ABOUT THE AUTHOR

John Regan was born in Middlesbrough on March 20th, 1965. He currently lives in the Acklam area of Middlesbrough.

This is the author's fourth book. The first – **The Hanging Tree** – was a gritty thriller, set in and around the Teesside area. His second – **Persistence of Vision** – a sci-fi/fantasy novel. The third - **The Romanov Relic -** a comedy-thriller

At present his full-time job is as an underground telephone Engineer at Openreach and has worked for both BT and Openreach for the past eighteen years.

He is about to embark on his fifth novel and hopes to have it completed sometime next year.

March 2018.

The author would be happy to hear feedback about this book and will be pleased to answer emails from any readers.

Email: johnregan1965@yahoo.co.uk.

OTHER BOOKS BY THIS AUTHOR

THE HANGING TREE – Even the darkest of secrets deserve an audience.
Sandra Stewart and her daughter are brutally murdered in 2006. Stephen Stewart, her husband, is wanted in connection with their deaths, having disappeared on the night of Sandra's murder.
Why has he returned eight years later?
And why is he systematically slaughtering apparently unconnected people?
Could it be the original investigation was flawed?
Detective Inspector Peter Graveney is catapulted headlong into an almost unfathomable case. Thwarted at every turn by faceless individuals, intent on keeping the truth buried.
Are there people close to the investigation, possibly even within the force, determined to prevent him from finding out what actually happened?
As he becomes ever more embroiled. He battles with his past, as skeletons in his own closet, rattle loudly. Tempted into an increasingly dangerous affair with his new Detective Sergeant Stephanie Marne, Graveney finds people he can trust, rapidly diminishing.
But who's manipulating who? And as he moves ever closer to the truth, he finds the person he holds most dear, threatened.
Graphically covering adult themes 'The hanging tree' is a relentless edge of the seat ride, exploring the darkest of secrets and the lengths people will go to keep those secrets hidden. Culminating in a horrific and visceral finale, as Graveney relentlessly pursues it to its final conclusion.

'Even the darkest of secrets deserve an audience.'

PERSISTENCE OF VISION – Seeing is most definitely not believing!

Amorphous: Lindsey and Beth separated by thirty years. Or so it seems. Their lives about to collide, changing them both forever. Will a higher power intervene and re-write their past and future?

Legerdemain (Sleight of hand): Ten winners of a competition held by the handsome and charismatic billionaire—Christian Gainford - are invited to his remote house in the Scottish Highlands. But is he all he seems and what does he have in store for them? There really is no such thing as a free lunch, as the ten are about to discover.

Broken: Sandi and Steve are thrown together. By accident or design? Steve is forced to fight not only for Sandi but for his own sanity. Can he trust his senses when everything he ever relied on appears suspect?

Insidious: Killers are copying the crimes of the dead psychopath, Devon Wicken. Will Jack be able to save his wife—Charlotte—from them? Or are they always one step ahead of Jack?

A series of short stories cleverly linked together in an original narrative with one common theme—Reality. But what's real and what isn't?

Exciting action mixed with humour and mystery will keep you guessing throughout. It will alter your perceptions forever.

Reality just got a little weirder! Fact or fiction…You decide!
Seeing is most definitely not believing!

THE ROMANOV RELIC – The Erimus Mysteries

Hilarious comedy thriller!

Private Detective, Bill Hockney is murdered while searching for the fabled – Romanov Eagle, cast for The Tsar. His three nephews inherit his business, setting about, not only discovering its whereabouts but also who killed their uncle.

A side-splitting story, full of northern humour, nefarious baddies, madcap characters, plot twists, real ale, multiple showers, out of control libido, bone-shaped chews and a dog called Baggage.

Can Sam, Phillip and Albert, assisted by Sam's best friend Tommo, outwit the long list of people intent on owning the statue, while simultaneously trying to keep a grip on their love lives?
Or will they be thwarted by the menagerie of increasingly desperate villains?

Solving crime has never been this funny!

Printed in Poland
by Amazon Fulfillment
Poland Sp. z o.o., Wrocław